Issue 15
June - July 2019

Heart's Kiss

Lezli Robyn & Tina Smith, Editors
Shahid Mahmud, Publisher

Amanda Pillar, Cover Artist

Published by Arc Manor/Heart's Nest Press
P.O. Box 10339
Rockville, MD 20849-0339

Heart's Kiss is published in February, April, June, August, October and December.

www.HeartsKiss.com

Pleaee refer to our website for information on how to submit material for *Heart's Kiss* magazine.

Available by subscription (www.HeartsKiss.com) or through your favorite online store (Amazon.com, BN.com, etc.).

ISBN:

FOREIGN LANGUAGE RIGHTS: Please refer all inquiries pertaining to foreign language rights to Shahid Mahmud, Arc Manor, P.O. Box 10339, Rockville, MD 20849-0339. Tel: 1-240-645-2214. Fax 1-310-388-8440. Email admin@ArcManor.com.

Contents

I0521354

OPENING EDITORIAL

by Tina Smith

It's always a wonderful feeling to read and prepare another issue of *Heart's Kiss*. And a time warp too. For example, while reading for June's issue it was cold and rainy and I was contemplating if I should make reservations for Valentine's Day or prepare a nice meal for my husband at home (spoiler—I usually choose homemade meal. Restaurants are nice, but too crowded on V-Day). Then the stories go on a long journey of formatting, copy edits, typesetting, more formatting, more edits. By the time we have a complete issue so much has happened and as I'm rereading the wonderful stories our authors have created, it transports me back to what had been happening when I read them first. Sadly, this time it reminded me that I read these stories when my grandfather was still alive and now he's gone.

It's the magic of a story that can bring us to places and recreate emotions we thought were buried. It reminds us we have so many things for which to be grateful. It reminds us of good times and bad. Romance is a versatile genre and it plays with our emotions and delivers us safely to a happy ending. It leaves us on a good note. Our authors each have a talent to do exactly that in their own unique way.

A few of our most exciting offerings this month are a longer treat for those who like to savor their fiction. *USA Today* bestselling author, Anna J. Stewart, has concluded her two-part novella *Lost and Magic Bound* and I was biting my nails wondering if Elya would be able to go through with her decision to offer herself for atonement. Anna also has some wonderful news professionally—a book she wrote for Harlequin is being made into a movie! We are delighted for her and lucky to have her writing for us. *Under the Solstice Moon* by Tonya D. Price was another fantastic second chance love story set in beautiful Greece. As a teen, Ava and her boyfriend broke up because she made an unfortunate choice. Now he's back just as she needs someone to lean on after her father's death and request in his will to carry out a task during the solstice moon. But is her past boyfriend who he seems?

We also have three new-to-*Heart's Kiss* authors Krista Wallace, Johanna Rothman, and Amanda Pillar. Krista Wallace has a cute contemporary-come-paranormal romance with a nurse who is having a bad day and a patient son of her patient who seems to keep showing up when she's at her worst—but that doesn't stop him from flirting his way into her heart in *Duchess Keeps her Head*. For a trip to the country, Rothman has a little cowboy tale about a woman who is afraid of horses and a man who is willing to help her through that fear. In the end *Queenie's Rescue* will surprise you and cheer for our characters. Amanda Pillar, *USA Today* bestselling author, adds more paranormal flavor to our magazine this issue with *Stolen Secrets*. Two demons may be rivals, but they soon find out they are also destined mates.

Welcoming back Olivette Devaux, we are gifted with her adorable story *Thor*, about a four-legged friend who manages to find himself in a custody battle between two homes and eventually these two men discover that's not all they have in common, but also a pretty sweet attraction for each other as well.

Last, we have our non-fiction offerings Julie Pitzel brings us a fantastic column in this installment of *You Read That?* This time she dives into the history and lore of our paranormal vampire heroes. Why are they so fascinating? She'll tell you, but don't get to close, they bite! C.S. DeAvilla has a new list of *Recommended Books* and Andrea Abedi shares her refreshing Green Lemonade recipe to help nourish our readers ahead of a thirsty issue filled with love.

Great stories transport us. They evoke emotion not only in our concern for the characters but in reminding us what has made us feel that way in our daily lives. It's healing. Rejuvenating. Comforting. And yes, sometimes sad. We strive to bring you all those things and more.

USA Today and national bestselling author Anna J. Stewart writes sweet to sexy romance for Harlequin's Heartwarming and Romantic Suspense lines, but paranormal romance is her first love. Early obsessions with Star Wars, Star Trek, *and* Wonder Woman *set her on the path to creating fun, funny, and family-centric romances with happily ever afters for her independent heroines. Anna lives in Northern California where she deals with a serious* Supernatural *and* Sherlock *addiction and tolerates an overly affectionate cat named Snickers. You can read more about Anna and her books at www.authorannastewart.com.*

LOST AND MAGIC BOUND

Part II

Warden of Time series

by Anna J. Stewart

From the moment Elya released her grip on Gareth, she felt herself fall. Seconds, minutes, hours, days…the unending darkness that had sucked her in howled against her ears as shapeless grey puffs of light drifted around and through her. The moisture on her face evaporated. Her clothes, soaked all the way to her skin, dried. In the distance, she heard Tyrus's distinctive montari whimper as he shifted in the pack on her back.

A bright blue light approached from a distance, slowly bobbing and weaving its way through the inky black, never slowing and only stopping when it hovered before her fear-wide eyes. She couldn't look away from the spinning depths of color playing out within its contained border, felt her mind relaxing, her body easing as it stopped fighting and simply surrendered to the decent. She blinked and, in that instant, the blue light pushed forward straight into her forehead.

She gasped. Her head snapped back. Her body locked, preventing her from moving. She could feel the warmth, a presence, encapsulate her thoughts, dragging her suddenly heavy lids closed. *Gareth.* Where was Gareth? It was the last conscious thought she had before she gave in, gave up, and sank into oblivion.

❖

Gareth's blood pounded through his body as he dived forward, digging through the sand that had dragged Elya and Tyrus away from him. The magic that pulsed back at him nearly drove him to his knees, but he remained upright. Guilt roared up inside of him. What had he done, telling her to trust the magic even he himself had lost faith in? The abject fear he'd seen flash in her eyes would haunt him to the end of his days. Fear he'd put there, by leading them into this place. By asking her to trust him. Panic surged through him, pushing the desperate need to follow her to bursting. The power built, circled, picking up speed and heat as sharp glass-like granules cut into his fingers, his palms as he dug deeper, further.

"It is not your journey to take."

Gareth spun, arms stretched out in front of him as he pushed the magic out in automatic defense. The golden-robed figure in front of him lifted a hand to block the blast of energy. The reflected wave knocked Gareth off his feet and sent him flying through the air. He landed hard on his back, his pack crushed under his weight, his body vibrating with the effects of his own, blood-sizzling magic.

The figure moved forward; the voice familiar in Gareth's ringing ears. With another wave of the man's hand, his head cleared. The aches and pain in his body eased. Air passed easily through his lungs again and he dragged in deep gulps and shielded his eyes as the figure moved over him and blocked the blinding suns.

"Still acting first and thinking second, I see."

That voice. Gareth shoved himself up on his elbows, disbelief crowding out the mindless desperation to follow Elya into the darkness. "Ijaro?" No. It wasn't possible. His old mentor was long gone, long dead. Or so he'd heard. But the amber eyes staring down at him, the crinkled ebony skin, the wide smile that conveyed both amusement and disappointment combined in his foggy mind to say otherwise. "It's not possible."

Ijaro made a tsking sound and shook his head. "In magic all is possible."

No, Gareth corrected. No, it wasn't. Because from the moment the sand curtained closed behind Elya's flexing hand, he'd lost her. No more of her thoughts in his mind, no more of the silent singing she'd been doing to keep herself moving through the razor rain that had driven them to these sand hills. No more…of her.

It was that absence, that…emptiness, that surged through him now and nearly drove the air from his body again. Dread locked around his heart. He'd hear her screams for the rest of his life. In his ears. In his mind.

In his soul.

He'd failed her. He'd lost her, left her alone. And worse than that? She'd left him.

"Self-pity and reflection will do you no good, Gareth. There was nothing you could do to prevent this. Her time of testing began the moment you set her feet on the path. You know this." Ijaro moved closer, leaning on an aged and warped walking staff. "Where she goes, you cannot follow." Ijaro looked up and closed his eyes. "She will be returned to you should she be deemed worthy."

The rain that had been driving them away from Larius and the Lurkers eased. The red clouds evaporated against a sudden gust of wind, as if they sky were purging itself of the toxic, poisonous rain. The fiery welts that covered the backs of Gareth's hands and face eased. The stench of sulfur and wet fabric evaporated into thin tendrils of smoke that drifted up and into the air.

"I would help you up, but I am afraid my old bones will not take the strain." Ijaro stepped back and Gareth struggled to his feet. "You are concerned for her."

"I am sworn to protect her. To guide her." Gareth forced himself to remain still, hundreds of questions swirling through his thoughts. "She is my charge."

Ijaro sighed. "Still not seeing what is right before your eyes. Tell me, Gareth. Is it Elya you are here for or yourself?"

And so, Gareth thought, his own trial began.

"Both." The admission broke free more easily than Gareth intended. More easily than he wanted, but then they both knew nothing, but the truth would pass through Gareth's lips as long as he was in his former mentor's presence. "I heard you were dead. Executed by Dracha for refusing to serve as one of his sorcerer defenders."

"A necessary fabrication to help save our people. The truth reveals itself when it is meant to."

The stooped old man clung to his walking staff as firmly as Gareth had attempted to cling to Elya. *Elya.* "Is she all right?"

"You were the one who told her to trust you, to let go. To fall." Ijaro's slight black eyes narrowed to the point of disappearing. "Do you no longer trust those who set you on your path?"

Gareth took a deep breath, reminding himself that it was foolish of him to believe even for a moment that the Zentali were not aware of his movements. Or that his motives and desires would not be questioned. He had removed himself from their ways, not to protect himself as some had accused, but to save them. "Elya's path is not my path."

"Is that so?" Ijaro tapped a gnarled finger against the smooth pale wood of the plain staff he held. "You neglected to answer my question. Do you no longer trust us?"

"For myself, yes." But for Elya? Witnessing her reaction to the revelation that he was Zentali had shown him his people had a long way to go before earning the trust of anyone not already entrenched with the race of sorcerers. She had been touched by Dracha and the darkness. A darkness most Zentali would have little or no compassion for. She'd been safe with him. But was she safe with his people? "I have given my word she will reach the temple safely. Whatever it is you have planned…."

Ijaro's normally placid, wrinkled face broke into smile nearly as bright as the twin suns in the sky of the Forgotten Realm. His dark skin glistened against the pale color of his robes and without moving, the beads of bells and crystals dripping from the top of his walking staff jingled in the sudden silence of the desert. "The questioning will take as long as it takes. These are uncertain times, Gareth. Those who pass through our land must be examined of their true intentions."

Gareth felt Ijaro's thoughts pressing against his, probing, digging deep for answers Gareth wasn't ready to provide. With a blink of thought, he inclined his head and locked the door in his mind.

Ijaro's smile widened as if in pride.

"Since when do you or the Zentali call the Presalas Valley home?" The last he'd heard the few Zentali who survived had taken up residence in the depths of the Scorian Forest far to the east. The endless, un-forgiving desert seemed a stark and troubling contrast to the peaceful land near the water's edge.

"Since Dracha's defeat. The temptations offered to our brothers did not stop with the exiles. We had defections up until the end. It was in our best interest to find new shelter once those who had dwelled with us left. Come. You shall wait with us while Elya is tested."

"She's not alone."

"Yes. We know. The montari pup will be waiting for you when we arrive." Ijaro stepped forward, pushed Gareth to the side and held out his hand, moving it in a circle until the sand of the hill Elya had been pulled into parted. Anger tightened his jaw at the effortlessness of the action.

"Intent, Gareth, is always the precursor to success. Desperation, guilt, fear," Ijaro turned his head slightly, "will never get you where you need to go."

Translation? Gareth had let his emotions cloud his focus. He'd been so focused on Elya, on losing her, she had moved beyond his reach. With a silent grumble of acknowledgement, Gareth followed Ijaro into the hill, wishing he could remain in the desert a while longer, under the warm rays of the suns to ease the settled chill in his bones.

It was the noise that struck him first. The noise of dozens—no, his eyes widened as shock turned to amazement—the noise of hundreds of voices laughing, shouting, speaking all around him. People. Animals, livestock and pets. While the suns vanished behind him with the closing of the sands, the radiant yellow of the light glowing far above the homes that had been built cast the people and their rustic dwellings in a glow that warmed Gareth's heart.

Men, women, and children of all ages milled about and as far as the eye could see. A village of sorts, safely locked behind the magical shields within the desert. A village where the spark of magic surged through his system, welcoming him. "Are they all Zentali?" Gareth's breath caught in his chest. He knew the answer before Ijaro spoke. "There are so many."

"With the portals being opened between realms, we have become a refuge." Ijaro moved more slowly than Gareth was used to, and he slowed his pace so as not to overtake his old mentor. "Each Zentali gives of himself or herself—"

"Herself?" Gareth nearly stumbled at the sight of an older woman entertaining a group of young children by making a collection of dolls dance in the air. "Females? There are Zentali females? But that's… impossible. The Zentali magic has only ever been passed from fathers to sons." Small stalls and wagons sat amongst the people, some filled with food, others offering tunics and gowns milled with glittering gold thread and laces of rich, tempting color. Hair weavers and magic makers, entertainers, and tradesmen plied their wares and talents as far as he could see.

"Magic finds a way." Ijaro cast him one of his irritating, knowing looks. "With the near eradication of our people, it seems the universe was not ready to let us go completely. I can only hope that in time we will not be forced to hide. I continue to believe that Callandra will one day offer us her forgiveness and allow us to live freely beneath the sky once more."

"I wouldn't count on that."

Ijaro stopped in front of a small dwelling. Gareth noted the Zentali symbols carved into the wooden door. The frame was just wide and tall enough for Ijaro to enter. Gareth had to duck.

"Do not rob an old man of his hopes, Gareth."

"Hope all you want." Gareth followed him inside. "Callandra will never change her mind about the Zentali." If she couldn't forgive her only son for what he was, she would never forgive strangers. Even if those strangers were, essentially, her own people.

"Spoken like the boy you were when you first arrived for my tutelage. Ah, this must be Tyrus." Ijaro leaned his staff against the wall beside the door as Tyrus ran toward Gareth. "He has bonded with you." Ijaro turned curious eyes on Gareth as he stooped down and scooped up the floppy-eared, big-pawed white pup.

"No. He's bonded with Elya." The relief that swept through Gareth upon holding the pup once more took him completely off guard. "You doing okay? Took a tumble, didn't you?" He scrubbed his hand deep into the fur between Tyrus's ears. "Where'd you leave your mistress, huh?" He pressed his forehead to the montari's and wished he could read the animal's thoughts. "What?" He didn't like the way Ijaro was watching him.

"He has bonded with you." The old man circled his fingers in front of Gareth's nose. "I see the light in both your eyes."

"That's impossible. I saw him bond with Elya. Montari only bond to one soul."

"Hmmm." Ijaro removed his robe and draped it over the simple chair by one of the windows looking out on the path they'd walked. "Tell me." Ijaro waved him deeper into the dwelling and motioned for him to sit on one of the cushions on the floor while he hobbled out of sight. Gareth watched, Tyrus still demanding his attention, as a pot of water on the oddly shaped stove began to boil. "Given what happened on your last journey, I wonder why you would answer your mother's call."

"Don't call her that." It was bad enough he'd uttered the word himself only a few days ago. A word he'd sworn never to speak again as long as he'd lived. "A mother doesn't banish her son to a prison realm, nor does she execute the man she claimed to love."

"A mother does what she must to protect her children." Ijaro returned with Elya's pack in his hands. He set it on the floor beside Gareth.

"Callandra murdered my father."

"Not everything is simple." Ijaro hobbled over to the stove to retrieve cups. "You will have tea and then get some rest."

"No. I want to see Elya."

"As stubborn as ever, I see." Ijaro shook his head. "You know the tests she faces. You know the ritual. You will do as you're told and wait until the test is complete. If she is deemed worthy, you will both be on your way with less than a day out of your time."

"Who are we to deem her worthy of anything?"

Ijaro started, surprise jumping into his eyes. "An excellent question, Gareth. We are who we were made. You care for her."

Gareth swallowed hard. To deny the claim would be to lie and that was impossible where Ijaro was concerned. "I will drink your tea. I will not rest until I know Elya is safe."

"We do not harm," Ijaro snapped in an uncharacteristic flash of temper. "For you to believe otherwise—"

"I will not rest until Elya is safe and back with me." He accepted the plain wooden cup and, sniffed. "If you've doctored this in any way…." Gareth waved his hand over the top of the cup, watched the liquid shimmer as he noted the various ingredients. Berrylin root, callapapa leaves, and Yennetta nectar.

"That you believe I would drug you so you would do my bidding is more a statement on your faith than my intentions." Ijaro sighed and poured his own tea. "You have been away from your people for too long, Gareth. You have lost your way."

Gareth drank, recognizing the familiar, spicy taste of the tea that had been part of his morning meals for countless years. "Until a few moments ago, other than Larius, I had no idea how many Zentali were left."

"Ah, Larius. The trouble you two would get into," Ijaro laughed. "The trouble his children will be."

A sick feeling crept into Gareth's stomach. "You know of Larius's children?"

"I know of all Zentali in this realm." Ijaro sat in a chair near the stove, groaned as he eased off his feet. "I am getting old, Gareth, but my gifts remain ever steady. The time is coming where we will need to move into the light. The darkness can only sustain us for so long. It's time for the Zentali to be free once more."

"Larius's children, they're both—" Fear for his friend, for his friend's children nearly choked him.

"They are." Ijaro nodded. "And will soon come into their powers. The question is, will this world accept them, or will we have another war on our hands?"

"No," Elya whimpered, trying to shut her eyes against the darkness, turn her face away from the memories flashing before her. But her body wouldn't obey. Her thoughts wouldn't. Flashes of her past sliced through her mind, agonizing stabs of pain she couldn't escape. "Please."

The mirror appeared, shifting through foggy memory and settling in front of her, its thick beveled frame glistening silver and tarnished black. She couldn't help but look, couldn't resist the pull as her reflection shimmered into view. A reflection, not only of who she was now, but who she'd been. As a child laughing and playing with Elian on the grounds of the temple where their mother had given birth to them. Where their mother had died days later leaving their father, a scholar devoted to the recording of the history of their people, to follow a

short three years later, of a broken heart. In the roaring wind-kissed silence, her memories, her most personal, played out before her. She saw them, through the tears, through the pain, she saw her parents once more, laughing together beneath the thick foliage of the goddess kissed gardens. Her father kneeling in front of their mother, his hands placed on either sound of her rounded stomach, her mother's hand stroking his hair as she hummed a tune that Elya herself had used to comfort herself for all her life.

"Mama." Elya's whisper cut through the bright image of her parents and flashed her through the next years. Elya growing into adulthood under the guide and tutelage of the goddess Callandra herself. Elian becoming a warrior and guard who would eventually help lead the rebellion against Dracha to victory. Elya, in those early first-blush days of love for Uryen.

A grey fog drifted across the mirror's reflection. Elya's stomach tightened and she whimpered again, wanting nothing more than to forget. *Not this. Not. This!* Would that she could travel back and prevent her naïve self from falling beneath the seductive promises of a man who had wanted nothing more than her magic and position. Even now, knowing what Uryen was, a Zentali corrupted by the promise of power and wealth, she felt her heart tip toward him. The handsome, fair face. The temptation in his eyes that had convinced her she was the only thing he desired. How had she been so foolish? How could she not have seen what he was? But she had seen. When it was too late.

Her image in the mirror was of what she had been—in her flowing robes, her silver hair spilling in long curls beyond her waist. Her face alight with the glowing promise of love and a future, a future outside the temple with a man who loved her above all others.

Uryen loomed behind her, that deceitful mask of a face, his hands moving up her arms to capture her shoulders and turn her toward him. The face she saw in her dreams, in her nightmares, met her gaze in the glass, razor sharp, dark and evil. Unscarred features, radiant eyes, and a touch as soft as the petals of a capralias flower. The sky darkened. Storm clouds moved in and around the image she saw in the mirror.

"No." Once again, Elya tried to look away. She didn't want to see any more. She didn't want to feel what he had made her feel. His kiss had enthralled her. His touch awakened her and when he'd taken her, when she'd given herself to him, only then did she see, did she know, the truth. In the deepest recesses of her mind she screamed. Elya watched, helpless again, as Uryen turned her to face the mirror, the black-eyed, vacant stare chilling Elya to her core as her silver hair transformed into the black of Dracha's heart. Uryen bent down, whispered in her ear. Even now, as she watched, she could feel the heat of his breath, the strength of his hands as he'd commanded her, abandoned her. Controlled her.

Elya's eyes blurred with tears that refused to fall. She was not that girl any longer. She would not, could not succumb to the memories nor to the shame they brought her. Not when she was so close to earning the right to forget them once and for all. Whatever this place was, whatever force was pillaging her mind, she would endure. She would reach the temple. She would surrender to their rituals and offer herself for atonement and the only peace she knew was possible for her.

She watched herself fade in the mirror. Relief cascaded through her until the faces of three women shimmered into sight. Elya's lips trembled at the sight of the MacQueen sisters, Clara, Nellie, and Amber, arms interlinked as they were dragged into a world they had no knowledge of; a world only they could save. Their screams, their protestations, their shock followed Elya into every dream, pushed her out of every restful sleep.

They were safe now, Elya told herself as if the thought alone could erase the darkness in her mind. They were back in their world, with the men they loved by their sides. They had survived.

As the reminder flitted through her thoughts, Elya's mind cleared. Just long enough for her to call out to the women she had nearly killed. If she focused, just enough, if she could only…. Every ounce of magic she possessed swirled inside of her. Her blood pumped. The chill on her skin faded beneath the warmth of her power. Her fingers twitched. Only barely. Only enough to catch her attention. Enough for her to focus on making them move. The pain screeched through her as her fingers clenched into fists. "I see them!" Her hoarse voice echoed into the unending darkness around her, the words cracking webs in the glass as she saw a valley appear before her. A valley with a thatched roof cottage and three, no, four red-headed women sitting in an endless garden of exploding color and life.

Life in the eyes of the MacQueen sisters and their…and their mother! "Shonna." The tears she'd kept at bay flooded her eyes again. The goddesses's daughter was alive! The three daughters she'd birthed were with her and…and each of them carried their own child. Amber, a boy, Elya knew in an instant. As strong and dark-haired as his father, Rivalin. Nellie would have a girl, with a smile as charming as Keane, who would love her without end. And Clara, the youngest. Elya's breath hitched in her chest. Clara, the youngest of the sisters, perhaps the strongest of the three, carried twins. A boy and a girl. Children of magic. They would all be children of magic. Children of the Goddess. "They're safe." Elya sobbed against the release of grief as her heart expanded with joy. She'd been told they were safe; told they'd returned to the lives they'd been snatched from. Elya had even partly believed but until this moment….

"Where'd you leave your mistress, huh?"

Elya gasped. Gareth! She'd heard Gareth's voice. She was certain of it. Elya pounded her fists against that which held her firm, twisted her head from side to side. "I'm here! Here! Let me…." She screamed in pain as she ripped her arms up before slamming them back down. "Let me go!" *Let me go back to him. Please. Let me go back to him.*

The mirror flickered. The image of the cottage in the valley shifting out of sight. The cracks in the mirror multiplied, the sound of strained glass cracking the silence, echoing into the darkness of the void which trapped her.

"I said," sweat broke out on her face as heat swirled inside her chest, "I said let me go!" She screamed the last word, the strength and magic shooting out of her and into the mirror. The glass exploded. Elya felt the freedom and rush of release as the bindings that trapped her vanished. She fell again, gently this time, as if she were an infant being lowered into a cradle. Her mind emptied. All the grief, all the sorrow, all the guilt, drained out of her. Finally. Her eyes drifted closed on a sigh. Finally, she could sleep.

❖

Gareth was loathed to admit it, but Ijaro had been right. He should have gotten some sleep. The exhaustion that crept over him was no doubt his body's reaction to the endless trek through the razor-rain and the unending desert hours before. His leg still ached from the wounds he'd received in the depths of the grotto despite the salve Elya had used. The guilt and fear over Elya being taken from him seeped through him like a toxic potion.

Ijaro himself had climbed onto the cot near the stove and fallen into a snoring slumber leaving Gareth to wander the small confines of the old master's dwelling with a growing sense of unease.

Unease that drew him outside and back into the village teeming with Zentali.

If he let himself, if he unleashed the magic stored within him, he could hear those who dwelled far beyond anything he could see. If he'd let himself, he would have known, far earlier than the moment Ijaro had appeared, that his assumption the Zentali had been eradicated was wrong. They had not only survived, they'd thrived. They'd multiplied. And here, hidden within the magical depths of the desert, they lived.

The pale pink sky above had dimmed. Torches flickered to life as he walked down the path he and Ijaro had traversed upon Gareth's arrival. How long had it been? Hours? Days? Time didn't seem real here. Nothing seemed real here. Every voice, every face, dozens, hundreds of them swarming around him, in his mind both invigorated and worried him. So many. There were so many of them, how could they possibly be safe while those outside the boundaries of the desert wished them gone.

The faint strains of string-plucked and fluted music danced against his ears as he strode through the crowd, taking in as much as he could. The laughter, the delight-sparked eyes. The smell of roasting meats and fresh-baked breads. Barrels of fruit and wine were offered up and bargained for as children— so many children—spun about their parents' and grandparents' feet. The sight of it all, the feel of it all, nearly drove him to his knees.

This, all this before him had been his father's dream, had become Gareth's dream despite him knowing it would never be possible. Except…it had been possible.

Knees shaky, he stopped beside a giant fountain where children splashed and laughed, tossing water into the air and turning the droplets into creatures from their thoughts. He tried to push his concerns for Elya aside as he splashed water on his face, along the back of his neck.

One young boy snapped his finger and water exploded up and spun, a rainbow of scales refracting against the torchlight from a nearby stall. Another girl, the boy's sister Gareth guessed, sent her own creature to soar around the scaled creature before plucking it into its talons and flying away.

"No fair!" The boy cried. "That was my…." The boy's attention froze on Gareth. Eyes as iridescent as a farrengold blossom locked onto him, then lowered. "Is that a montari?" The boy dropped to the ground a few inches from Tyrus, awe and wonder lighting his face.

"It is." Gareth turned and sat on the edge of the fountain, water dribbling down the back of his collar. "His name is Tyrus." At the mention of his name, the pup turned a couple of circles, darted in and around Gareth's feet then plopped down a hand's reach from the boy. "I'm Gareth."

"I'm Kalen. That's my sister Sebali. I've never seen a montari up close." The boy tilted his head. "Does he bite?"

"Not to my knowledge. He belongs to a friend of mine."

"He's very pretty." Sebali, who had a good three inches on her brother, knelt down, her long dark hair twisted in intricate braids down her back. The orange and yellow dress she wore shimmered in the pale pink-light of the make-believe sky. "Does he like to be petted?"

"I'm not sure. Do you, Tyrus?" Gareth leaned down and gave the pup a good scratch. Tyrus looked up at him with something Gareth swore looked like a smile, then dropped to the ground, belly up and wiggled closer to the children. "I will take that as a yes."

After a good few minutes of attention, more children joined them, followed closely by some adults, who seemed far more interested in Gareth than Tyrus. He bowed his head in silent greeting, crossing two fingers from each hand in front of one another. The greeting, a silent acknowledgement of his

Zentali heritage, erased the tension he felt growing among the crowd.

"Told you he was Zentali," Kalen elbowed his sister.

"I'm waiting for my friend," Gareth told them. "Her name is Elya." At the mention of the name Tyrus bounded away from the children and returned to Gareth, jumping up to press his feet on Gareth's knees. *Yes, I know,* Gareth pushed into the pup's mind. *I miss her, too.* "Perhaps one of you knows where she might be?" It was a long shot, but his anxiety over her whereabouts, while it had eased a bit, was flaring up. He reached behind him, scooped up a palm full of water and, as he faced them, transformed the liquid into an image of Elya. "Have any of you seen her?" He drew his hand across, watching expressions for any hint of acknowledgement.

"I have!" A little girl, who looked no older than six, broke free of her father's hold and raced forward. She stood at Gareth's knee, and lifted both tiny hands to either side of Elya's face. Gareth watched as Elya's image was replaced with that of a lush garden surrounded by rocks and sand. "That's where I saw her. While I was waiting for papa outside the bread stall near our home. Papa? It's the pretty lady I saw sleeping."

"I assumed she was making up stories." The girl's father stepped forward and lifted his daughter into his arms as Gareth stood. "I'm Aladair. This is Isa."

"Do you know where she's talking about?" Gareth asked

"I do." Aladair bowed his head, his long, nearly white hair dropping around his shoulders "I can show you."

"I can show him." Isa kicked free and once she was on the ground, reached for Gareth's hand. "Come Gareth. Come with me."

"I—all right." He found himself laughing as he had to bend over to take her hand. She was a little bit of a girl, with fine blonde hair and blinding blue eyes. "Tyrus." He called over his shoulder and had the montari hurrying after them, leaving disappointed children behind. "She seems to know where she's going."

"Isa always knows where she's going." Something in Aladair's voice caught Gareth's attention, but he refrained from enquiring further as Isa dragged him through the throng of people, down and around the edge of the village.

"Almost there." Isa sighed. "This is a long way, papa. I think I will need something to eat soon."

"We'll eat when we get home," Aladair assured her.

"I was playing just there." Isa stopped and pointed to a clearing just beyond before she stomped into the grass. "I heard her talking, like we were talking. She sounded scared. Then sad. She was asleep again when I found her. There she is." Isa tugged Gareth's arm and gestured toward the small lake. "She's very pretty," Isa declared. "Don't you think so, Gareth?"

He did think so. He motioned for Tyrus to stay with Isa and Aladair and approached Elya's still form. She was lying in the grass, hands placed over her heart. Her silver hair lay splayed around her, her face utterly and completely serene beneath the pink sky.

Gareth stood over her for a moment, his heart barely beating. Was she breathing? Was she…alive? He dropped to one knee and with a trembling finger, brushed her pale cheek.

The moments he waited seemed an eternity. His mind raced wondering what he would do if his urging her to let go had led her to her death. Not out of obligation over the oath he'd sworn to guide her, but because of the overwhelming acceptance that without her, the world—any world—would be a far darker place.

"Isa, we should go." Aladair's voice sounded behind Gareth.

"No, Papa. I want to meet the pretty lady."

Gareth looked over as Isa came over to stand beside him. She laid her tiny hand on his shoulder. A warm glow of energy drifted down his arm and out his fingers. The pale-yellow light sank into Elya's still form and had her fluttering her lashes. When Elya's silver eyes opened and she stared, confused, into the odd sky, Gareth looked to Isa.

"Papa says I can only use my magic for good. She was lost. Sad." Isa inclined her head, frowned. "So sad. I did good?"

"You did very good, Isa." Gareth covered her hand in his. "Thank you."

"I did good, Papa." Isa's pretty little face seemed paler than before and when her father came to draw her away, she swayed a bit.

"You did perfectly, Isa." Gareth didn't miss the flash of grief that crossed Aladair's thin features.

"Gareth? Oh! Tyrus." Elya gasped when the pup landed in her lap before she could sit up. "I had the oddest...." Her hair spilled around her shoulders, her eyes bright and lively for the briefest of moments. "Where are we?"

"Safe." Gareth shooed the pup away and drew her to her feet. "What do you remember?"

Her face clouded and she gripped his hand. "Everything. I remember everything. I heard you." She reached up, touched his face, a bit of wonder in her gaze. "I heard you and then everything was all right. What am I doing here? Where are we?" She repeated and now that her mind seemed to be clearing, her voice sounded stronger.

He could lie, Gareth thought. They would soon be leaving. He wouldn't have to keep the secret for long, but looking down at her now, as if seeing her with new eyes, grateful eyes, he knew he couldn't. "With my people," Gareth told her, bracing himself for the reaction. "With the Zentali."

"The Zen...." Elya's brow furrowed and she stepped back, looking beyond him to where Aladair and his daughter stood. "They're Zentali? She's...I don't understand. I thought all Zentali were male."

"Magic finds a way." Ijaro's words found their way out of Gareth's mouth. "This is Aladair and his daughter Isa. She's the one who led me to you."

"You both must be tired and hungry." Aladair stepped forward, a suddenly exhausted Isa in his arms. "Will you join Isa and me for evening meal?"

Gareth hesitated. They had already lost time. They could make it up, but not if they lingered too long.

"Please?" Isa held out her hand to Elya. "Please, pretty lady?"

Elya stepped away from Gareth and took Isa's hand, clutching it between both of hers and bringing it to her heart. "We would be honored, little one." She bowed her head. "Thank you."

Gareth's heart swelled at the compassion in Elya's voice.

"Please, follow us. It's not far," Aladair urged.

Gareth scooped Tyrus off the grass, stopping him from chewing on the thick greens, but when he placed his hand on the small of Elya's back, he felt her shudder and barely contain a sob. "What is it? Are you hurt? Did something—"

"It's not me," Elya whispered, her eyes filling with tears. "It's Isa." She pressed a hand hard against her heart. "She's dying."

❖

Elya stayed close to Gareth as they followed Aladair and Isa to their dwelling. The wonder of the village, the surprise at the sheer number of people milling about as they wound their way through crowds and market stalls and homes, didn't settle amidst the tumultuous emotions circling inside of her.

"How do you know?" Gareth asked under his breath. He slipped his arm around her waist and drew Elya close as they maneuvered through the crowd.

"I could feel it. I told you I was a healer, back at the Temple. One of them at least. I never committed to it completely, but I was trained and was told I had the instinct of one. I can't explain it exactly, but when I took her hand, I just knew. In the way her blood flows in her veins. The way her heart beats. It's...." Elya shook her head.

Gareth didn't respond due to the fact they'd reached their destination. They followed Aladair's lead and removed their shoes, the rounded opening brushing the top of Gareth's head as they stepped inside.

"I'm sure it's not what you're used to." Aladair turned slightly to address Elya.

"It's lovely," she told him as he laid Isa on the mattress beside the fire and drew the blanket up over her. Tyrus struggled in Gareth's hold and when his feet hit the floor, the pup padded over to the little girl and hopped up next to her. Isa smiled, her eyes drooping when she reached out to pet him.

"She'll sleep a bit." Aladair motioned for them to join him across the solitary room where he quickly cleared the square wooden table. "Using her magic exhausts her. More so every day." His smile was quick and didn't reach his brilliant amber eyes. "I hope you don't mind stew. I've got some fresh bread from Chantari. She's Isa's favorite baker. She's even given her lessons at times."

"Aladair." Elya caught his hand when he turned away. "What's wrong with her?"

He shook his head, allowed Gareth to push him into one of the chairs. "No one seems to know. It's...

Ijaro has done all he can, but they think it's her heart. The magic weakens it."

"Like what she did for Elya?" Gareth asked.

"Yes." Aladair. "She can't stand to see anyone sad or suffering. One touch, one thought, and she can bring them such joy. Such happiness. I've tried to stop her from using it, tried to tell her why, but, I can't. Helping, healing people, it's who she is. It's who her mother was. I cannot deny her."

Elya swallowed hard. "Your daughter has a very special gift." Why, why, was she so at a loss for words? The peaceful slumber she'd drifted into had been blissful. Devoid of memories, of regret, of pain. And the light that had surrounded her, a soft yellow, cloud-like light that lifted her back to this world, had felt like comfort and perfection personified. And then…she'd seen him. Gareth.

Gareth who was everything Uryen wasn't. Gareth who had led her, protected her, tempted her. Gareth who would never lie to her or deceive her.

"Has Ijaro mentioned a binding?" Gareth asked. "Just long enough to help her regain her strength?"

"He has." Aladair nodded, hugging two wooden cups against his chest. "And I considered it, but that would be selfish, wouldn't it?"

"I'm sorry, but what's a binding?" Elya looked between the two men.

"It's when a Zentali's powers are too much for him. Or her." He glanced over at Isa who had fallen asleep. "Especially in one so young. It's not done frequently, but often it's for those with great power. More power than their bodies can withstand. It turns off the magic, just until they're of an age when they can be more easily processed."

"It seems a simple solution, doesn't it?" Aladair managed a thin smile. "Simply turn off that which is hurting her. But doing so would change who she is. That magic is a part of her. I'd no sooner take that away from her than I would change the color of her eyes."

"Even if that means losing her?" Elya asked.

"Yes." Aladair nodded. "Even then."

❖

Elya didn't know her heart could hurt any more than it already did. Being forced to replay what had happened to her had nearly ripped her in two, but now, sitting outside Aladair and Isa's dwelling, a cup of hot tea cupped between her palms, she'd found she had an entirely hidden part of her heart that had been attacked now. Isa had awakened long enough to have something to eat, but it was clear she would soon be sleeping again. She'd given her father a hug and patted gentle, small hands against his back when he'd held her tight. "Don't worry, Papa. I'm feeling better."

"Losing one with such promise is difficult."

Elya glanced up from the tea and found an old man with dark skin standing nearby. His gold cloak shimmered beneath the darkening pink sky. His fingers were wrapped tight around the walking staff at his side. "You must be Ijaro."

Ijaro's mouth split into a wide grin and he hobbled forward, lowering himself onto the narrow bench beside her. "Gareth is most efficient with his information. You have recovered from your—"

"Inquisition?" Elya tucked her feet under her.

"As accurate a term as any, I suppose." Ijaro heaved a heavy sigh. "You are the first who passed through, Elya, High Priestess of Callandra. You are the first we have trusted. And do you know why we trust you?"

"I haven't the faintest clue." How could they when she couldn't trust herself? She knew what she was capable of.

"Because you trust him. Even knowing what he is. You trust Gareth."

"He's proven himself trustworthy. It doesn't matter that he's Zentali."

"Precisely my point, child. I have lived many, many years. Far longer than you can comprehend. I've watched our people be hunted, executed, banished, and berated. I know the damage a few of our kind have done. To Callandra herself. To the Realms. To you."

Elya glanced away. "I've spent enough time in my past today, if you don't mind."

"What Uryen did is unfathomable to a true Zentali. To cause such damage, not only to your body, not only to your mind, but to your soul, there is not enough magic in the universe to heal those wounds."

"No," Elya whispered. "There's not."

"At one time you blamed us. Blamed all of us for what was done to you."

Guilt closed her throat. "Yes."

"But you do not any longer. Because you have met a true Zentali. Gareth is the best of us, Elya. Misguided at times. Frustrating and stubborn. But at his core, he is what we all strive to be.

That you would see through your own experience to understand who he truly is shows you are a woman far more intelligent and promising than the Goddess you serve."

Elya squeezed her eyes shut, shook her head.

"Your devotion confuses you." The bells on Ijaro's staff jingled when he set it aside. "You are conflicted. We saw it in your mind, felt it in your heart, during your…interrogation."

A laugh bubbled inside of her. At the time, she'd thought being made to relive her past was tantamount to torture. Now she had to wonder if it had opened her mind to thoughts she never would have entertained before. "I was raised in temple. From the moment I drew breath, Callandra was my world. She taught me kindness and compassion, acceptance and love. And yet." Elya leaned over and looked at the people who circled and played and entertained in this hidden world. "And yet she exiled all of you. Continues to keep you all from living in the light of the world she oversees. Why? How can she do that?"

"It is a question I have asked myself countless times. Perhaps it is time someone asked that question of her."

❖

"Did you want to talk about what happened?" Gareth waited until Ijaro led them to a private dwelling near the garden where he'd found Elya. Tyrus seemed to approve, doing a good sniffing and exploring job before curling up on the hearth beside the lit fire. It was quiet, secluded, sparsely but efficiently decorated, but most of all had the only thing Gareth was thinking about right now: a bed.

"What do you mean what happened?" Elya looked at him as if she had no idea what he was talking about. "Oh. You mean when Ijaro and his invisible cadre probed my deepest thoughts in order to determine whether I was a spy for Callandra? No. I really would rather just forget that." She laughed then, the sound almost hysterical and he wondered just how

much further she could be pushed before she broke. "Forget. Everything comes back to the same thing, doesn't it? Wanting to forget the past."

"We can still turn back." Gareth tried to keep the hope out of his voice. Her resolve had been cracked. He could feel it. He'd heard it in her voice as clearly as he'd heard the conversation between her and Ijaro. "You can still change your mind."

"No." She drew her fingers across the delicate bouquet of flowers someone had left on the table by the stove. "No, I can't."

"Forgetting your past doesn't only mean forgetting what happened with Uryen and Dracha."

"I know that."

"It means forgetting everything that's happened on this journey. It means forgetting Tyrus. And Aladair and Isa. It means forgetting this place. The grotto. All the good things that have happened to you as well." He stood behind her, not touching her, not daring to despite it being all he wanted. The sight of her, the smell of her, the wildflowers and rain, the way her fingers brushed against his when she thought he needed comfort. "It means forgetting me."

He heard her soft intake of breath before she turned to face him. The pain on her face, the agony in her eyes nearly broke him in two. "Gareth. Stop. Don't."

"I'm a selfish person."

Her sad smile only made him hurt worse. She lifted her hand, brushed the backs of her fingers against his cheek. "That's not true."

"It is." He caught her hand, drew her fingers to his mouth and kissed them, one by one. "I abandoned my people, abandoned my magic, because I couldn't move beyond the past. I stayed angry, so angry at my mo—at Callandra. At my father for leaving me to fight on my own. At Ijaro for never seeming to understand what I wanted or needed. I locked myself away because I didn't want to feel anymore. I didn't want to feel anything." His free hand slipped down the side of her body, over the curve of her hip, drawing her closer. "And then you arrived, turning my world upside down, shaking me loose of my self-pitying seclusion. Because of you, I've found my people. I've been reminded of the fact that I'm not alone. I haven't been. From the moment I saw you."

Her eyes filled, happy tears, he thought as her lips curved. Elya reached up, clasped her hands behind his head and drew his lips to hers.

"Don't leave me alone, Elya," he whispered against her mouth. "Stay with me. Be with me. Tonight." He kissed her, slow. Deep. Pressing her softness about every edge of him, pressing his mind against the edges of hers. "Tomorrow." He drew away far enough to look into her searching eyes. "Always."

"Gareth." His name was a whisper on her lips. "I can't give you everything you're asking for. It's not in me. That woman, she died a long time ago."

"No, she didn't." How could she not see? How could she not understand?

"She did." She spoke as if explaining to a stubborn child. "And as perfect as always sounds, I can only offer you tonight." She rubbed her mouth against his, tightened her hold. "If that's not enough, tell me now." She moved her hips in a way that tightened every part of him. "It's your choice."

A choice that would rip his soul in two. Would it be easier, having made love to her, knowing he never would again? Could the memory of her be enough? Or should he walk away, never having known how perfect, how absolutely perfect, the rest of his life could have been. Would he spend another day not imagining her walking into the kitchen, the early morning suns streaming through his window? Hearing her humming that lullaby he'd bet she didn't know she hummed. Seeing her full with their child, a wondrous combination of their magic and love? "I want more than one night." He squeezed his eyes shut, willing her to change her mind. Willing her to see the past didn't have to define the road either of them took. "I want more."

"I know. But this is all I can give you. Tell me now, Gareth. Before neither one of us can walk away." She traced her fingers over his lips, raised up on her toes and pressed her body more firmly against his.

She was wrong. He didn't have a choice. He'd never had one from the moment he opened his front door. "Tonight, then." He bent down, lifted her in his arms, and carried her to bed.

❖

"This is beautiful." Elya's statement, along with her feather-light touch as she drew his hand closer to inspect, drew Gareth out of a light sleep. Never before had he felt such…contentment. Being with her, holding her, making love with her, had brought him to the edge of a precipice he hadn't known existed. He'd stepped off, willingly. And he continued to soar.

Gareth drew her tighter against him, unwilling to take the chance she'd vanish from his bed. She traced a finger along the interwoven symbols in the tattoo. "Where did you get it?"

"My father." Gareth waited for the bitterness to descend, but instead he found himself remembering the ritual with a smile. "A few weeks before he was… before he died, he and Ijaro performed our people's ascension ritual. It's when we accept our Zentali heritage and our place in the tribe."

"How old were you?"

"Eight? Nine?" He'd stopped counting once his father was gone. "It's not usually performed until much later, but I understood later he wanted to witness the ceremony. That he was the one who did the markings makes them all the more powerful."

"Oh?" She lifted his hand to her lips, brushed her mouth against his fingertips.

"Mmmm." He nuzzled her neck, inhaled the deep, intoxicating fragrance of her hair, of her skin. Of her. "It's always felt as if I carried a bit of him, a piece of his magic with me."

"Tell me what they mean. The symbols."

He groaned. "I'm not entirely sure my brain is capable of conversation at the moment."

She turned her face, looked over her shoulder. "Tell me."

He would never be able to resist any request she made of him, would he? "Each symbol represents a Zentali tenant, our code of conduct. Do only good. Seek out truth. Protect and defend the outcast. Listen in the dark."

"Listen in the dark? What does that mean?"

He rolled her under him and pressed his mouth to hers. "It means sometimes more can be said in silence if you only listen."

She laughed, wrapping herself around him. "I think you made that last one up."

"Maybe." He nipped at her, slipped his hands down the sides of her naked body and heard her groan. "We can discuss it later." He kissed her again. "Much, much, later."

❖

The silence woke her.

The stark, blissful silence of utter contentment and peace. It didn't feel right. Didn't feel…normal. But she welcomed it, nonetheless. It wasn't just the quiet of the Zentali village, or even in the dwelling where she lay locked in Gareth's embrace, Tyrus's montari snores echoing against the walls.

It was the silence of her soul. The screaming, the agony, the pain she'd carried inside of her from the moment the spell had been lifted from her many cycles before, was…gone. She rubbed her hand between her breasts, waiting for it to descend again, waiting for the suffocating guilt and grief to surround her heart and squeeze, but it didn't come. All that did was the warm, comforting sensation of the man sleeping beside her. Gareth.

The man she…loved? Did she even know what love was? She'd thought herself in love before, but that had been a trick. A spell. No. No, it was time she accepted responsibility for what had befallen her. It had been her own naiveté, her desire for more than a simple life of devotion to the Goddess. She'd wanted to love. She'd wanted to be loved.

Something Uryen had known from the beginning. He'd used that to offer her everything she'd ever dreamed of. Before sending her catapulting into an unending nightmare of darkness and forced service to a power determined to end everything she cared for.

She turned her head, looked at Gareth sleeping beside her, curled into her. Surrounding her. Lifting her hand, she memorized this moment, would keep it close for as long as she could. She knew, with absolute certainty, she'd made the right decision to continue on her journey to the Temple of Atonement. She was at peace with it.

And yet something had jolted her out of the most restful sleep she'd had for ages.

She'd been dreaming again. Not the nightmares. Nothing about Dracha or the portals or the mind-prison she'd been locked in by Uryen. Elya bit her lip, squeezed her eyes shut and tried to remember. There had been a glow, yellow, soft. She'd been in the temple years ago. A young girl, not even ten yet, but she'd been training with the healers for more than two years at that point. At times the ill or infirmed were brought to them, but in this instance, she'd accompanied Thalia, one of Callandra's most trusted advisors, to the home of a young family whose daughter was seriously ill and dying.

Every nerve in Elya's body fired. She'd forgotten all about this day. Forgotten about Thalia, the family. The child. How had she done that? She'd watched as Thalia, with her sleek silver hair and deep silver-grey eyes had examined the girl, probed her mind with her own, then her body with gentle, caring hands. Empathic transitioning, Thalia had murmured. A transfer of energy, from one person to another. The young girl's life force was being drained by her magic. A magic she used to help others in need. A magic Thalia declared must not be lost.

"Isa." The girl had been suffering in the same way as Aladair's daughter. Isa, who had brought Elya back to Gareth. Isa, who was dying by the minute. Perhaps by the second.

She couldn't let that happen. Not when there was the hope…. Elya held her breath. Was it possible?

Beneath the blanket, Elya gently lifted Gareth's arm from around her and slipped from their bed. Across the room, Tyrus's head shot up, a whine emanating before Elya hushed him with a finger to her lips. She swore the dog pouted at her before he went back to sleep. Quietly, quickly, Elya dressed, drawing on the long tunic and pants. Not wanting to take the time, she forewent her shoes and instead grabbed her pack, slung it over her shoulder and, after a regretful glance at Gareth, she left the dwelling.

The rough sand bit into the bare soles of her feet as she hurried through down the darkened, winding path. The village had gone as quiet as a tomb, but the torchlight guided her down the short alleyway to Aladair's dwelling where she rapped her knuckles on the door. It took another two knocks before he responded. "Aladair. I'm sorry. I know it's late." Her apology came out in a rush as Aladair blinked at her. He was disheveled and pale and squinting in confusion.

"More like early. Is everything all right?"

"I need to come in." She didn't shove her way in, despite wanting to. "I need to see Isa."

"She's having a bad night." Aladair shook his head. "I just got her to sleep. I don't want to wake her up."

"Neither do I. I promise." Energy she hadn't felt in ages surged through her as he stepped back and allowed her to enter. She dropped her pack and faced him. "Do you have a pair of shears or a very sharp knife?"

"I—what?" Irritation flashed in his eyes. "What's going on?"

"I know what's wrong with Isa." She bent down, sorted through the collection of medicinal herbs and aids she'd brought with her.

"That's not possible. Not even Ijaro—"

"I've seen it before. Once, a very long time ago. When I served in the temple. Aladair, I've seen it be cured." Only now did her stomach start to tighten into knots of unease. She had no idea if it was going to work, if she could remember all that was needed, but it was worth a try. She owed it to them, and she needed so badly to do something good before she bid goodbye to this life. "Please let me try."

"I—" Hope flared in Aladair's eyes before reason stepped in. "Is it dangerous?"

Elya understood what he was asking. Welcoming them into his home was one thing. Trusting a priestess of Callandra, a woman who had done her best to rid the world of his kind, with his only child, was quite another.

"There is no danger to Isa," Elya said without hesitation. "Please, Aladair." She saw it, the silent acquiescence before he nodded.

"Perhaps we send for Ijaro?" Aladair said as he retrieved a pair of shears.

"There's no time. She's getting worse, isn't she?" Elya drew her hair over her shoulder. Quickly, she braided it and tied off the end.

"Yes." Aladair frowned. "How did you know?"

"Do you have any elamata berries?" She rattled off a few other herbs and flowers she hadn't thought to bring with her.

"I'm not sure. If I do, they're in the cabinet in the back room."

"Please get them. We need to brew a tea." She gathered up her own bottles and after setting them on the table by the stove, set a large pot of water to boiling.

"You've seen this work before?" Aladair added the last of the ingredients to the collection on the table.

"Yes." Elya surrendered herself to the memories pushing forward. She could see Thalia, the girl under her care, as clearly in her mind as she could see Aladair standing beside her. As she dropped ingredient after ingredient, she murmured words long remembered, long forgotten. "I've seen this malady before. A long time ago. I wasn't much older than Isa is now. But I helped with the healing."

"The healing? You mean it worked?" Aladair looked as if he dare not hope.

"The last I heard, the girl was married and had a family of her own. It wasn't an easy healing. It took a lot out of…her." She stumbled over the last word.

"What can I do?" Aladair asked.

"Nothing." She reached out and rested her hand on his arm for a beat of a moment. "Your trust is all I need. I promise you, on my life, on Gareth's, I mean your child no harm."

"I wouldn't think otherwise," Aladair insisted. "Gareth trusts you. That's enough for me."

Of course. Even without him here, Gareth was still helping her. Elya pressed her hands against her forehead, calmed herself. "I do need you to promise me something, Aladair."

"Anything."

"Whatever you see happen, you need to let me finish." She gathered a bowl, into which she placed the sheers, a cloth, and the jar of necabar buds, the potent and fragrant flowers that grew around the lakes and rivers of all the realms. "I need to enter a trance and I'll need your word you will do exactly as I tell you when I tell you. I will not be in a mental state to argue with you."

Aladair nodded and followed her to Isa's bedside. She lowered herself to the ground, set the bowl beside her and, taking a deep breath, stretched out her arms and lay her hands gently on Isa's stomach. "When the tea has been boiling for half an hour, pull it off the stove, cover it and wait until I ask for it. You'll need two cups. One for me, one for Isa."

"One for you?" Aladair asked. "Why will you need the tea?"

"No more questions." She looked at him, and for a moment, saw Gareth where he stood, a disapproving frown on his rugged, handsome face. Whatever happened to her, he would understand. At least she hoped he would.

She picked up the shears and, placing her hair between the blades just below her shoulder, cut until the braid dropped limply into her hand. Aladair gasped, but she silenced him with a look. She placed what had been her only physical source of pride into the wooden bowl and doused it with farrengold oil. She whispered the incantation as easily as if she'd heard it hours rather than years before. The braid began to glow, the white and silver shifting along the tresses as the oil seeped in. Elya lifted the braid free and, with a gentle touch, coiled the braid around Isa's head. She took a moment to smooth a finger down the little girl's ashen cheek. "Stay strong, little one. We'll get you home now."

"Elya?" Aladair's voice sounded as if from a distance. She didn't respond. Couldn't. Not as the magic began to swirl and the power surged. She closed her eyes, took a deep breath, emptied her mind and let go.

❖

For a man used to sleeping alone, Gareth felt oddly out of sorts when he woke to find Elya gone. The mattress beside him was cool to the touch, the blankets drawn up around him as if placed with care.

Tyrus let out a huff of air and bounded up onto the bed, but instead of circling and settling into his mistress's spot, he tapped his paw against Gareth's hip. "What's going on?" Gareth reached out to give the pup pat. "Where is she?"

Tyrus barked once, that sharp bark of warning Gareth had heard only once before, at the grotto before Larius had appeared.

Gareth sat up, the blanket falling away. "Elya?" He called her name again as he pushed out of bed, noting her most, but not all of her clothing was gone. Her shoes remained. But she'd taken her pack. "Elya!" He searched the rest of the dwelling; the small back privacy room, pulled open the front door to check outside. "Where in the Realms—Ijaro." He nearly jumped a foot out of his skin. "What are you doing here? Have you seen Elya?"

"Only in my mind," the old man said with an edge to his voice Gareth had heard only a few times before. "Dress. Quickly. We will go to her together. I can only hope we are not too late."

Dread curled through him, hot and slick. "Too late for what?" He gathered up his clothes and was dressed in moments, dragging on his boots and didn't bother to lace his tunic completely before he'd scooped Tyrus off the bed and joined Ijaro outside. "What's going on, Ijaro? Is she in danger?"

"Only from herself." The old man moved fast, fast enough to both impress and concern Gareth. "We should have seen it, seen beyond her desire to leave her life behind. Our own bias blinded us to what she truly seeks."

"What she truly seeks? What does that mean?"

The bells on Ijaro's walking staff grated on Gareth's nerves.

"She seeks a life serving a higher purpose. Beyond her service to Callandra. Beyond her attachment to you. Her willingness to sacrifice herself in exchange for forgiveness that is not warranted may very well end your journey before its completion."

Sacrifice herself? "Elya does not wish to end her...." He couldn't finish the statement. Not because the thought terrified him, but because it wasn't true. Her journey to the temple, her desire to have her memory erased so she could start again, was tantamount to precisely what Ijaro said. Gareth had never met anyone so caring, so empathically connected to the world around her, to virtual strangers, than Elya. He had no doubt she would willingly give up her life if it meant saving someone else. "She wouldn't have left me without a word." Even though every moment he'd had her in his arms had felt like a goodbye, she wouldn't have denied him one last look. One last kiss. One last touch.

He shivered. Would she?

"She has not left you. Not yet."

Ijaro turned down the path to Aladair's home and in that moment, he understood. "Isa. This has to do with Isa." Gareth ran the final steps, Tyrus nipping at his heels. Even before he could knock, Aladair swung open the door, his pale face tight and strained as he let them in.

"I can't get through," he whispered. "Gareth, I'm sorry. She said she could...." He motioned to Isa's bed where his daughter lay on her back, her cheeks flushed bright pink, the grey pallor of her skin that had been growing worse even as they'd shared a meal with Aladair, gone. But still she slept. And on the floor, beside her, Elya sat, hands splayed over Isa's stomach.

Barely breathing. Still as death. "I don't know what to do."

"The tea. Where is the tea she had you brew?" Ijaro set his staff against the wall, closed the door, and walked to the cooling pot.

Gareth, frozen where he stood, watched as Elya's lashes fluttered against her pale cheeks. "Elya?" He dived for her, caught her as she fell to the side. He cradled her head against his shoulder as she tried to open her eyes. "Elya? Talk to me. What did you do? What's wrong?"

"Make her drink this." Ijaro pushed a wooden cup into Gareth's hand while he sat on the bed beside Isa and drew her up to drink from her own cup. "All of it, Gareth. And then another. It is a restorative."

Gareth didn't understand, but he did as he was told, holding the cup to Elya's lips. Relief swept through him when she opened her mouth and drew the tea in. Her breathing sounded ragged, as if her lungs were full of water. Her arms lay limp at her sides, as if her bones had been removed. When the cup was empty, Aladair was there to refill it and then Isa's cup until the pot was nearly empty.

"Papa." Isa's voice broke through the forced silence of the room. "Papa?"

"Isa!"

Gareth lifted his gaze from Elya's face as Aladair dropped to his knees on the other side of the bed. Isa was sitting up, her face flush with color and life. Her eyes sparkling against the fire burning nearby.

"She's warm," Aladair whispered, moving his hands along Isa's face, down her arms, back up to cup her face. "You feel warm."

"I am warm, Papa. The magic doesn't hurt anymore." She scrambled forward and into his arms. Her long silver hair billowing around her shoulders and down her back.

"Elya." Gareth drew a hand down her shorn hair, remembering what it felt like to lose his hands, but bury his face, in the silky length.

"You'll need to drink this every morning, Isa," Ijaro said and urged Isa toward him so she could drink more of her tea.

"I know. Elya told me. In here." Isa tapped her head and knelt on the bed beside Ijaro and took the cup from him. "But only for a little while. Until her magic binds with mine." She shook her head and looked down at her hair. "Papa, look! It's like Elya's."

"Yes, it is," Aladair whispered.

"Her magic?" Gareth looked down at Elya as she stirred in his arms. She blinked open her eyes. Eyes that seemed cloudy and dull. "Elya," he whispered. "What did you do?"

"What I had to." She lifted her hand, brushed it against his. "Don't be angry. I won't need my magic much longer." Elya turned her head to where Isa sat between Ijaro and Aladair. "Now it's hers. Now she'll live."

But would Elya? Gareth looked to Ijaro as Elya drifted off once more. The silent question earned him only a slow shake of his mentor's head. Ijaro didn't know.

"Can I help her?" Isa asked as her father went to get her more tea.

"You cannot, little one." Ijaro told her. "But it speaks to your heart that you wish to try. "Elya is the one person your magic will not work on any longer. She must find her own way through this. She must find her own way back."

❖

For so long Elya had only wanted one thing: a long, dreamless sleep.

The prize came with a price. A price she wasn't sure of until she opened her eyes and found herself looking up at the ceiling of the dwelling she'd shared with Gareth. Gareth.

She tried to sit up, but her body wouldn't obey. Her head spun as the blood drained from her face. She shivered, groaned, and turned over on her side, curling up until the nausea subsided and she thought she could open her mouth without emptying her stomach.

"Drink." The cup that was pushed under her nose made it worse. She would have shoved it away if she hadn't been hauled up and the cup braced between her lips. "Drink it all, Elya."

Gareth.

The sound of his voice eased her, and she did as he said. The bitter, tangy liquid slid down her throat, leaving her feeling exhausted but alive. Alive. She sighed, pushed the cup away and looked up at him.

"That's right. You're alive. Surprised?"

Guilt surged but she bit it back. "A little." She pushed her hands into her hair, shock shooting through her when it disappeared at her shoulders. Then she remembered. The ritual. The spell. "Isa?"

"She's fine. Perfect. Healed." Gareth remained where he was, standing statue still like a temple guard, the chill in his amber eyes making her shiver once more. "You should have told me what you were planning."

"You were asleep."

"It doesn't take much to wake me. I'd think you'd know that after our night together."

He set her cup aside, sat down beside her, then planted his hands on either side of her hips. "You didn't wake me to tell me because you knew I'd stop you."

"I—" She was going to argue with him, going to tell him he was wrong, but the challenge in his eyes clearly dared her to lie to him. "Yes. I needed to do it, Gareth. I didn't want to argue about it."

"Ijaro said there was a way to perform the spell without you draining your magic. If we'd done it together, if you'd asked for help—"

"Gareth." She lifted her hand to his face, cupped his cheek in her palm. "Is it not enough for me to say you were right?" Some of the anger vanished from his gaze. Enough that she saw the hurt behind it. "I knew what the price might be, and I was willing to pay it. How could I not when it meant that beautiful little girl might live."

"I am thrilled Isa is going to be all right," Gareth said. "But how is it you have so much compassion and empathy for everyone but yourself? You've left your family because you believe you tainted them with your presence. You left the temple because you believe you betrayed them. You walked away from Callandra even after she told you there was nothing to forgive. And now you all but ended your own life because you didn't think it worth living any more."

His accusation stung, not because it wasn't true. But because it was. She'd been willing to give up her life if it meant Isa would live. To leave this world be-

hind by saving another? There was no higher calling. "That wasn't why I did it."

"No. You did it because you're afraid." His words shot out like ice, sharp, cold, and stinging. "You're afraid of what happens if the Temple of Atonement accepts you and allows you to proceed with the ritual and you're afraid of what happens if they don't. You're just afraid, Elya. Of living the life you've been given. Of living a life that's not yours. Of living a life with me."

"Gareth." It had never occurred to her...never crossed her mind....

"Healing Isa, surrendering your magic, risking your life? That was a potential way out of all of it. I was wrong before. You really are a coward."

"Gareth!" She sat up as he bolted off the bed and began to pack their bags. She thought he of all people would understand.

"You've been asleep more than a day. We have two days to reach the temple. If you still want to go?" He glared at her, but behind the anger, behind that hurt she'd seen before, now she saw disappointment. And perhaps the faintest sliver of hope. "Are you still going to the temple?"

"Yes." Her whisper barely reached her own ears. "Yes, I'm still going."

"Fine." He tightened the strap on his bag, picked it up, and walked out the front door.

"You will return." Ijaro stood before Gareth and Elya, that determined albeit devious grin on his ancient face. "Gareth, you will return."

"I will. Yes." Gareth bowed his head, offered the Zentali sign and tried not to notice how Elya fidgeted beside him. He'd spent the last few hours in the presence of his mentor, listening, perhaps for the first time in a very long time, to what the Zentali had before them. "Unless you all move on from this place."

"You have always had it in your power to find us," Ijaro told him. "Perhaps now you will be open to it."

Yes, Gareth thought. Perhaps he would be. He'd been surprised to find most of the village had turned up to bid them farewell. Perhaps he shouldn't have been given word of Elya's healing of Isa had reached every ear. Speaking of Isa, Gareth bent down in front of the little girl who stood in front of her father, her new silver hair braided in intricate patterns in much the way Elya had once done her own.

"You take care, little one." He reached out a hand only to have her throw herself into his arms and cling to his neck.

"I will miss you," Isa whispered in his ear then, when she pulled away, she bent down to pat Tyrus. "And you." She stepped over to Elya, who crouched in front of her and gave her braid a gentle tug, a small smile curving her lips.

"It's prettier on you."

"Thank you for saving my life."

Elya embraced the little girl, hanging on, Gareth thought, a bit longer than she'd planned.

"You are welcome with the Zentali any time, Elya." Ijaro said loud enough for all to hear. "We owe you a debt that can never be repaid. But, perhaps this will be a start." He turned and flashed open his hand. The sand that made up the road whirled and cycloned up, swirling into a portal of golden granules. "Your detour through the valley cost you much time. You are more than three days from your destination. I give you back two of those days. I cannot send you up the mountain pass, but I can get you to it. Go. And be safe, my children." Ijaro nodded to both of them and Gareth watched as Elya moved ahead of him and without looking back, stepped through the portal, Tyrus clutched in her arms.

"You know how to find me, too," Gareth told them before he followed. The obligation, the responsibility he'd shirked out of resentment and anger, resettled around his shoulders and seeped into his soul. If he couldn't have the future he found himself wanting with Elya, he would find one with his people. A people he would fight for. Even if that meant going up against the mother who wanted them all dead. "You have only to call and I will come. That is my vow. I am Zentali. For now. For always." After another bow, another smile of approval from Ijaro, Gareth walked away, and followed Elya.

❖

"So this is it." Elya stood at the base of the mountain and looked up. And up. And…. She let out a harsh breath. "How much further is it exactly?" She lowered Tyrus to the ground and tried to keep her

tone light. The tension between her and Gareth was only getting worse, but instead of pushing her toward changing her mind, he was only proving she'd made the right one.

She was no longer a girl who believed in fantasy and sweet promises whispered in the night. Those promises never came true and only led to heartbreak in the end. She'd had enough of that. She didn't want any more.

Even if Gareth did make her believe it might be possible. But possible wasn't enough. Not any more.

"No more than half a day's journey." Gareth strode past her, earning a whine of discontent from Tyrus who was clearly wanting to take the lead on the path before them. "I suppose we'll be arriving early after all."

"Still no bonus points, though, right?"

"No." Gareth didn't even look back at her. "No bonus points."

"Okay, then. May as well get started." She looked behind her, saw the rugged rocky path leading into a grove of farrengold trees outlining a crystal-clear lake glistening in the mid-afternoon suns. Far in the distance, the glint of what had become the Forgotten Realm's main city caught her eye. For a moment, she let her mind drift and open, reaching out for Elian in the way she had when they were children. But there was nothing to be found. Nothing to connect to. Tears blurred her eyes and she looked away, moving to follow Gareth, only to find him standing behind her.

"You can't connect with him any longer, can you?"

"No." She cleared her throat. "No, I can't. I forgot…I suppose I forgot how reliant I'd become on my magic." And without it she didn't feel quite whole. Didn't feel quite like herself. Ijaro had given her little hope it would ever return. She'd stayed connected to Isa for too long, drained herself too much. The embers she'd hoped to retain had drifted out of her like ash, vanishing in the air. "I never told him goodbye."

"So it's a pattern, then?"

She glared at him. "It was his wedding day. I didn't want to leave him with a bitter memory to cloud the joy."

"How magnanimous of you."

"You don't get to judge me, Gareth. Not when you've spent more than half your life ignoring a people who could have used your help. We all make the decisions we have to make. Whether they are mistakes or not."

"Not going to argue with you there," Gareth said. "Except to say I'm choosing to make up for those mistakes rather than letting someone make me forget them. We'd best be moving, otherwise we'll be spending the night on the mountain."

He said that as if it would be a bad thing.

"Yes," he said, without any pretence of having listened to her thoughts. "It would be."

"Get out of my head," she snapped.

"Make me." He glared at her over his shoulder, the dig at losing her magic hitting its target and making her flinch. "As I thought. Let's go."

The trek up the mountain made their journey through the dessert feel like a training session. It wasn't the path that made it difficult, although that had its obstacles with overgrown vines, enormous tree roots, and squelching mud. It was the incline, which went from flat to steep in the space of steps. And speaking of steps, Gareth finally stopped to take a break at the base of stone stairs that curved up and around the side of the mountain for as far as she could see.

Nausea swam in her belly as the air grew thin. She withdrew one of the parcels of food the village had given them, parcels that were brimming with more food than they could eat in a week. But she sank silently to the ground, her pack clutched in front of her as she breathed a sigh of relief.

"You should have told me you were tired." Gareth sat on one of the rocks nearby, Tyrus sitting, waiting patiently for Gareth to unwrap one of the chunks of meat Aladair had insisted they take. While the dog gobbled and Gareth unwrapped, Elya drank one of the bottles of water, then started a second.

"I didn't think I had to *tell* you anything," Elya told him. "Ijaro said I was fine to travel."

"He probably did not expect us to make the entire mountain path in one day." He glanced around, eyes guarded.

She withdrew a round, glossy ethyla fruit and bit into the sweet, juicy yellow flesh. "Are you going to tell me what lurks on the mountain or are we waiting to be surprised?"

His lips twitched and she took that as a good sign. "Ghosts."

"Is that meant to scare me?"

"It should." Gareth took a bite of homemade bread loaded with nuts and seeds.

"The dead don't haunt people, Gareth. And I can't imagine they stick around once they've passed on, either."

"Didn't say they were the ghosts of the dead." Gareth seemed to be looking anywhere other than at her. "It's the ghosts of the living we need to worry about. Our ghosts." Now he flicked his gaze to hers. "Have any of those?"

She swallowed hard, wiped her hands on her pants. "Can't be worse than what Ijaro put me through."

"I wouldn't bet on it."

It was then she remembered he'd been on this journey before. "What did you see? Your last time through?"

"My father. He made sure to let me know how disappointed he was in me." Gareth reached for his water and drank.

"Because you denied your Zentali past?"

"I've never denied it. I simply didn't embrace the past few years. Hard to do when people want you dead because of it, including my own mother."

"Your mother?" It was the first time he'd spoken of her and she could see instantly, he regretted the admission. "Who was she?"

"Is. She's still alive." He waved a hand as if to dismiss the topic. "Doesn't matter. She sent me away with my father when it was clear what I was."

"Sent you away. Is she of royal blood? Did she have that power?"

Gareth looked at her for a long moment, then shook his head. "She did. She does. And no. She's not of royal blood. Are you ready to start the climb?"

Elya looked up the staircase and sighed. She'd never be ready, but her energy had rebounded. "How long will you stay. After we get to the temple?"

"Long enough to complete my duties and see you're safe."

"Okay." Long enough for him to forgive her or perhaps come to some acceptance as to why she was doing what she needed to do. "Gareth?" She got to her feet, reached out and caught his arm as he pulled on his pack. "It's not you. You do know that, don't you? My decision to see this through, it has nothing to do with you."

"Yes, I know." His expression didn't flicker from one of resignation. "And that's the problem, isn't it? You call out if you get too far behind or if you need to stop. Tyrus? Stay close to the mountain side."

Tyrus barked when Gareth patted his hand against the stone of the mountain then bounded up the stairs ahead of them. Unsure what to say to him, unable to come up with a response, Elya did the only thing she could do. She slipped her pack on her back and followed him up the stairs.

"I think I'm going to die." Elya's wheeze broke through the top of the path with enough force to part the trees. Gareth and Tyrus were waiting for her, where the trees thinned, and the sun dipped low on the horizon. "Please tell me we're nearly there."

She dropped onto the ground and she swore her lungs screamed.

"Afraid not." He pointed up the arching grove of trees to the east. "The old path is grown over. New one through there. Takes us a bit out of our way, so another quarter day? Perhaps more."

"Awesome." Why did only a few days feel like years? "So, we're stuck here for the night?"

"Looks like." Gareth watched her with a guarded gaze. "We can eat a decent dinner, get some sleep, and start out first thing in the morning."

"Sounds like a plan to me." She didn't move. She couldn't move. Every muscle in her body ached to the point of throbbing. Even her hair hurt. "I'll help get things set up in just a minute." Her eyes drooped and she smothered a yawn. "Just give me a few…" she trailed off and dropped right into sleep.

Elya.

She shook her head against the whisper of her name against her ear.

Elya. Wake up. I have something to tell you.

Don't want to. She tried to roll over, to burrow under non-existent covers, but the ground was hard and the pack on her back was heavy, preventing her from moving. Go away.

Elya!

The voice snapped through the darkness and she shot up, terror clawing through her along with realization. She knew that voice.

Uryen.

She sat up. Her pack vanished. Her clothes had been replaced by the scratchy, tailored, suffocating fabrics of the other world. On her feet were pointed, spiked shoes that pinched her toes. She drew her fingers through the jet-black hair that spilled around her shoulders. Bile rose in her throat. Where was she? This wasn't the mountain. Gareth was nowhere to be seen. Not among the shelves of endless books in the tiny, cramped room. No. She wasn't here again. It couldn't be….

She stumbled for the door, pulled it open and ran down the narrow hall. A hall that continued to grow longer and longer and….

You're mine, Elya. You always have been. You always will be. You cannot escape me. I will search endless worlds for you. Run all you like, I will be with you.

You will not! Elya kicked off the shoes and resumed running past doors and hallways and shelves of books that trembled beneath the magic pulsing around her. You're dead! Dracha killed you! I saw it!

You saw what I wanted you to see. What Dracha wanted you to see. I am still here, Elya.

She looked over her shoulder, stumbled and turned to catch her balance. Hard hands caught her arms, hauled her up so she could look into the eyes of the man—of the creature—who had stolen every bit of her away. She screamed and with one mighty shake, she surfaced.

"Elya, wake up!" Gareth shook her again, hard, and her teeth rattled.

"I'm awake." Her voice shook as she tried to push him off. "I'm awake." Tyrus pushed his way between them and wedged himself on her lap, licking her face and nuzzling her neck. "It's alright. I'm awake."

Gareth released her, but not before she saw he was as shaken as she felt. "You were screaming. What did you see?"

She pushed her hair out of her face. "I don't remember," she lied. There was no point in telling him the truth. There was nothing he could do about the paths her mind took and besides, it was clear she needed to step away from him completely, in every way. "Just a nightmare, I guess. I'm fine, Gareth, really." She forced a smile onto her lips and, after dislodging her pack, stumbled to her feet to help him with the food. But there, in the back of her mind, she heard Uryen's voice: taunting, terrorizing. Terrifying.

She wouldn't be sleeping tonight.

❖

One thing Gareth had learned about Elya, almost from the moment they'd met. She was a terrible liar. He could always see it, the flicker of remorse that flashed in her eyes. The way she tucked her hair behind her ear without even realizing it. Whatever she'd dreamed had scared her into silence while they ate, gave Tyrus a workout chasing sticks they threw, preparing for bed.

His arms, his heart ached for her. Nothing he'd said, nothing they'd done had changed her mind about reaching the temple or about going through with the ritual that would erase all memory from her mind. She lay inches from him, turned on her side so he couldn't see her face, but he could tell by her breathing she didn't sleep. Even without prying too deeply into her thoughts he could feel the fear pulsing off her despite the exhaustion.

She was in pain. She had been from the moment they'd first met, but after being with her, after loving her, after falling in love with her, he could feel it as acutely as he felt his own, sharp, piercing, agonizing.

He shifted closer and without a word, slipped an arm under her and rolled her into him. "Tell me," he whispered against her hair.

She shook her head, her breath trembling out of her. "It's not your concern."

"It is." He tilted her chin up, looked into her silver eyes and hoped this wouldn't be the image he remembered for the rest of his life. "I love you, Elya."

She squeezed her eyes shut and tried to move away. "Don't say that," she whispered.

"You don't believe me."

"It's not a matter of believing. I can't trust my own feelings, Gareth. I want to love you. I want to believe there's something beyond this journey for us, but I cannot. Not when I can still feel him inside of my mind. Manipulating me. No matter what I do, no matter how hard I try, he's still there."

Gareth stroked her arm, puzzling the pieces together into some image that made sense. "He's dead, Elya. You told me yourself you saw him die. He only holds the power you continue to give him."

"Does the same apply to you?" Her hand clenched in the fabric of his shirt, as if telling herself she'd gone too far.

"What do you mean?"

"Your mother. You've never forgiven her for killing your father or for banishing you. Have you moved past that? Have you forgiven her?"

Gareth's hand stilled. A door he'd been hoping to keep closed opened. All he wanted from Elya was for her to trust him enough to believe; for her to realize there was a way, other than erasing that which made her so unique, so perfect. Perhaps with his own confession, he could break through that wall she'd built around herself. "I'm not sure I can ever forgive Callandra for what she's done. For what she continues to do by denying my people their right to exist and live free, peaceful lives."

He knew the instant the words sank in. Elya sat up, ripping herself free of his hold and, a hand braced on his chest, stared down at him. "Callandra? She's your mother? But…that's not possible. Her children, all of her children except for Shonna, are all—"

"Dead. Yes, I know. That was made abundantly clear to me when I was secreted away in the night by her guards." That was his nightmare; reliving that night, when he was barely more than Isa's age, the sounds of screams, the spatter of blood marring the pristine temple walls as he was led away by strangers' hands into the darkness that would never lift. "It was a group of Zentali who were responsible. Under Dracha's orders, maybe even under his control, they cast the spell on the guards who were responsible for their deaths."

Tears filled Elya's eyes as she reached a hand to his face. "Gareth. I am so sorry."

"Your blind faith in her is misplaced, Elya. Your devotion, while admirable, isn't deserved. Loyalty should be earned. Faith should be built, not taught. She had my father killed, Elya. For nothing more than being what he was born. She would have done the same to me had she the chance."

"I don't believe that. I *can't* believe that. Gareth, there must be more to this. The Callandra I know would never—"

"Stop, Elya." He shook his head, keeping his voice gentle. "Nothing you say or believe is going to change what happened. She did what she had to in order to protect herself and the world she'd built. She has kept my people, kept me, from living our true lives. How can any of the Zentali be free as long as she's declared them outlaws of the realms? That should show you who she truly is. It's who I see whenever I look at her."

"And yet you agreed to guide me to the temple at her request." Elya clutched at his hand as he stroked a finger down her cheek. "Why? Why would you do that if you hate her so much?"

He'd gone this far. There was no reason to lie to her now. "I did it on the condition it would be my last time." He'd be free of any obligation he had to his mother, the Goddess Callandra. But now he'd be trapped by another woman, by Elya, by the memories of what they'd shared. And the promise of what they'd lost. "My first trip to the temple was much the same as yours, Elya. I wanted nothing more than to forget all that had happened to me. My father, who my mother was, that I was hated and despised by anyone and everyone around me who was not Zentali. I made this journey, I prayed for the oblivion you seek."

"What happened?"

He hesitated, wondering if his words might finally be enough to convince her she was making a choice based not on hope for the future, but on fear from the past. "The Guardian of the Temple declared me unsuited. My intentions were not pure. It was deemed I was looking for an easy escape rather than an acceptance of fate. A fate I had yet to meet." Was Elya his fate? It was possible, if not for her determination to walk away from him, away from all that made her Elya, High Priestess of Callandra. "My rejection made me uniquely qualified to be a guide. And now, with you, my obligation will be over. One way or the other."

"Are they going to reject me?"

"It will depend on the Guardian's recommendation." His soul cried out at the unfairness of it all. "Do you truly see no other way for yourself, Elya? Is this truly what you want? To forget all that has passed, your family, your friends. The temple. Callandra. Tyrus? Me?"

"If there was a way to do this and remember you, I would take it in a heartbeat," Elya whispered. "But I cannot trust myself any longer, Gareth. The last time

I trusted my feelings people died. They suffered. All because I couldn't see the truth of what Uryen was. If he is still a part of me, even within my memories, then I can never truly believe he's gone. And I fear what may still live deep inside of me. I will not take the chance I would hurt more people, Gareth. I will not." A solitary tear escaped her control before she leaned down against him, curling into him as he tightened his hold. "My magic is where it should be. With Isa, who will use it only for good. That part of me is at peace." She took a shuddering breath. "The only part left is my soul."

Before the suns reached their zenith the next afternoon, Elya and Gareth stood before the wooden gates of the Temple of Atonement.

Anxiety mingled with relief as she curled her toes in her boots. She had come so far and yet the journey now felt as if it had happened in the blink of an eye. Gareth stood beside her, looking up at the simple pair of doors between them and her new life.

He reached out for the rope attached to a bell, but she caught his arm, drew his hand back and held it against his chest. "You aren't going to try to talk me out of this again?"

His faced her, drawing her forward and lowering his lips to hers in a kiss so gentle, so tender, so soul-achingly perfect, she sobbed when he pulled away. She wanted to cling to him, to lose herself in his embrace once more, to hold on to, but for how long? In minutes, hours, days, she would have no memory of him or their time together. "I love you, Elya." His whisper brushed against her ears and seeped through her like the warmest of balms. "I only wish it were enough."

He stepped free of her hold and pulled the rope. The bell echoed around them, through the trees, up into the sky peeking through the endless branches and flowers. Birds burst into flight and the skittering of animals sounded. The creak of hinges had her stepping back as the doors in front of her opened toward them.

"Elya." Gareth stepped back, motioned for her to go in.

"You aren't coming?" Her heart pounded so hard she felt it might explode. She never considered he wouldn't be staying at least long enough to recuperate from their journey.

"Gareth has only one task left to complete."

Elya spun toward the woman who spoke. Her tall, thin frame was hidden in the thin silky fabric in the color of the sky after a summer storm. She had no hair. Wore no adornments other than a tattoo encircling the upper part of her right arm. Simple leaves and flowers that reflected against the sun.

"I deliver her in safety." Gareth bowed his head as Tyrus stood at his feet, looking between Elya and him. "The journey has been completed."

"It has indeed." The woman bowed in return. "Welcome, Elya, daughter of Callandra. I am Pontame and will be your companion for the coming time." Additional figures, men and women, emerged from the billowing gardens within the confines of the temple. Stepped out of the stone buildings simply constructed. A circular pit in the center of the temple burned bright with fire, a well of spring water nearby. Fire and water, opposites and compliments. Together they brought life and sustenance, Elya recalled from her time in Callandra's temple. "It is time for the Guardian to make his decision. Has Elya been deemed worthy for the ritual? Is her intention pure? Is her reasoning sound?"

Elya searched the crowd for this Guardian Pontame spoke of, but none of the other priests or priestesses stepped forward to speak.

"The Guardian approves this woman."

Elya spun at hearing Gareth's voice, at absorbing the words he spoke. "Gareth?"

He looked beyond her; his eyes forcibly vacant as he swallowed hard. "She has passed the tests of fortitude, generosity, empathy, and faith. She is deserving of consideration and will serve you well upon completion."

"Gareth." Tears blurred Elya's eyes. "It was you? All this time…." Her voice broke. When he finally met her gaze, she saw the love in them, the grief. The sorrow.

"You wish to keep the montari with you?" Pontame placed a gentle hand on Elya's back.

Tyrus barked once but remained standing between Elya and Gareth. She bent down, held out her hand and sobbed when Tyrus approached, pushed his floppy-eared head into her hands. She lifted him into her arms, held him close and closed her eyes when he licked her face.

Instead of answering, she took the few steps to the gate where Gareth stood, and offered him the pup. "You belong together. Remember me kindly, Gareth. Forgive me for not being stronger."

He accepted Tyrus, tucking him firmly in his arm to prevent the pup from diving back at Elya. "Be well, Elya." He bowed his head as the gates began to close. Before she lost sight of him, he looked up, his amber eyes glistening. "I love you."

The gates closed between them.

In the days that followed, Elya's determination to see the ritual through found new depths. Not because the memories of Uryen and her own betrayal of her people continued to haunt her, but because of the emptiness swirling inside of her. Everywhere she turned, she saw Gareth, saw Tyrus, saw…promise. And for someone without hope, there was no greater torture.

"Your sadness grows." Pontame said one morning once the early meal was concluded. "Are your preparations not going well?"

"You would need to ask Haltus about that." The meditation exercises she'd been required to learn didn't seem to be doing her much good and only frustrating her tutor. "He says the council has yet to decide what my new role will be within the temple."

"It sometimes takes many months for the decision to be made." Pontame led the way down the narrow, stone path to the garden behind the main structure. The smaller stone ones acted as private dwellings for the nearly two dozen occupants of the Temple of Atonement. Elya's was closest to the temple itself, a simple room with a bed, a chair, table, and a window which overlooked the most abundant of the floral gardens on the grounds. With the cloudless sky and the cool breeze, this place was the epitome of perfection and offered her all the quiet and solace she could ever wish for.

And yet….

"You have yet to settle your thoughts, child. Come." Pontome guided her to a hand-carved wooden bench situated under a lush farrengold tree, its delicate blooms glowing in their usual light. "You are frustrated and wish this to be over."

"Yes." She'd learned her first day that untruths were considered disrespectful and not tolerated. "I came for a new life. A new beginning. But it feels as if the old one followed at too close a distance."

"Your heart is conflicted. That delays the process, Elya. Only without conflict can we truly see the path before us. We take our obligations to granting those a new life with great reverence. The Goddess Callandra demands it."

"Does she?" With as much time as she'd had to think, she'd been giving a lot of attention to Callandra and her own years in the Temple. The ancient texts that had once offered her much comfort now felt tainted. That the woman she'd loved, the woman she'd served willingly had nearly killed her own son, murdered his father? It felt like a betrayal of faith.

"You are angry with her." Pontame inclined her head, her stark dark eyes questioning.

"I am."

"Despite her approval of your journey."

"One act does not negate others. What she did to her son, to his father." Elya swallowed around the bitterness. That anyone would hurt Gareth in the way Callandra did had been eating away at her for days. "I will never understand it."

"Would you like to?" Pontame offered. She reached into her pocket and withdrew a smooth, white crystal. "This is the crystal of truth. We use it sparingly as the truth is often painful, both to see and understand. But we have agreed you are in need of it. If it is answers you seek, answers that will clear your intent, it is yours to use."

"What if the truth only leaves me with more questions?"

"The truth often does." Pontame pressed the crystal into her hand, closed Elya's fingers around it. "Empty your mind of all thoughts, Elya. All fears, all worries, all anticipation. Let go of regrets and wishes and dreams and let your mind take flight."

Pontame's voice drifted away as Elya surrendered to the pulsing in her hand. Behind closed eyes the darkness gave way to the light, the familiar, radiant light of the temple where Elya had spent most of her life. But the light faded. Darkness descended and when Elya's eyes adjusted, she found herself behind a pillar, deep in the recesses of the tunnels below the temple. In the prison cells thought long abandoned.

"There is nothing that can be done." The man who spoke stood in shadow, his voice unfamiliar. But the woman on the other side of the steel bars, the woman with her hands gripped tightly around them, was all too familiar. "The order has been given, Callandra. You cannot protect me now."

"You gave them no choice." Callandra's accusation slapped out at Elya, who stepped out of the darkness. "You gave me no choice. You confessed to treason, Jartho."

"To save our son. The son you are unable to claim as your own."

The son Elya missed so much she hurt.

"A son who will now hate me forever because I allowed his father to be killed."

"It is either lose me or lose both of us. You've failed the Zentali, Callandra. If you'd only listened to me, if you'd accepted us for who and what we are, my people would have never looked to Dracha for hope."

"I will pay for that mistake for eternity," Callandra whispered and for the first time in her life, Elya saw the goddess cry. "Let me save you. Let me secret you and Gareth away where I know you'll be safe. I will use all my powers…."

"He is gone, Callandra." Jartho stepped forward and covered Callandra's hands with his. "I sent him to Ijaro before I surrendered to the guards. I cannot tell you where he is. I do not know."

"I can find him if I so choose." Callandra announced.

"And what will your people do with the son of a confessed traitor?" The patience in Jartho's voice was more than Elya could bear. The honor, the loyalty Jartho showed for his people, for his son, left her trembling. "There is no way to stop this, Callandra. There is no plan to be hatched, no solution to be found. I've taken the precautions necessary. Gareth will protect my people. You've lost your other children. Do not lose another."

"Shonna lives," Callandra protested. "She's under the protection of my most trusted warriors."

"But she will never return. Keep the one you have left safe. He is the best of both of us, Callandra. Ijaro believes *he will save my people and yours. Is it not worth your pride to ensure his destiny?"*

"It wasn't pride."

Elya spun, the gasp escaping her lips as the scene before her vanished and Callandra stepped out of the shadows. The sadness etched on her delicate features reminded Elya so much of herself. "Gareth doesn't know, does he?"

"That Jartho sacrificed himself for his people?" As Callandra moved the world shimmered into sunlight, ocean waves crashing far in the distance, the temple pillars surrounding them like sturdy soldiers against the elements. "He does not. His anger towards me keeps him safe."

"And the Zentali? Does your hatred toward them keep him safe as well?"

If Callandra was surprised at Elya's accusation, or her tone, she didn't show it. "My feelings toward the Zentali are complicated."

"But why have them at all?" It didn't make any sense to Elya. Callandra was a goddess. Her powers unmatched. Her control of the Realms complete. What could possibly…. "You're scared of them." It was the only explanation she could find. "You're threatened by them."

"I was." Callandra winced. "Much to my shame. I listened to the wrong people. Allowed myself to become poisoned against them. By the time I realized my mistake, my second mistake," she added with a sad smile. "It was too late. There are too few left to ever hope to make amends."

Elya froze. Her mind raced. Callandra didn't know about the Zentali? But how was that possible? She knew everything about…"Gareth." He was protecting them. She hadn't seen the extent of his power, but he was the product of a Zentali and a goddess. He would easily have the ability to shield them.

"What about him?"

"You need to tell him the truth." Elya's voice snapped through the air. "He needs to know."

Callandra shook her head. "My son—"

"Your son has been basing his entire existence on a lie. A lie you and his father concocted to keep him safe, but instead you locked him in a prison of resentment. You have no idea who your son even is, do you?"

"Tell me about him," Callandra suggested. "What don't I know?"

"He's kind. Compassionate. Protective and loyal. If he gives his word, he keeps it. He will never turn his back on anyone in need and he will fight until his dying breath to defend that which he believes is right. He loves his people. He might not want to, he might not willingly choose the difficult path, but he will walk it when called upon. He's the best man I know. He's the man I—"

Callandra inclined her head. "He's the man you love."

Elya's heart skipped a beat before a flood of warmth washed through her body. "Yes." In that moment, all the distrust, all the grief and regret melted away, leaving only the hopeful promise of Gareth's face. His touch. His warmth. "You knew."

"I suspected. I've never had one of my priestesses speak to me in the manner in which you have, Elya. I recognize Gareth's influence well enough. But as far as telling him—I cannot. What if I'm wrong. What if he doesn't believe me or accept what I'm saying? What if—"

"What if you just take the chance and try?"

Callandra inhaled deeply as she considered the horizon. "I will if you will."

"I, what? No. No, I've already made my choice." Elya frantically tried to pull her feelings back, but it was no use. She was standing on the edge of a cliff of decision. Now she had to decide whether to jump.

"When you make yours, I will make mine. Be well, daughter." Callandra brushed gentle fingers on her arm. "Be well."

The crystal fell from Elya's hand as she opened her eyes.

Pomante leaned over to retrieve it, a knowing expression on her kind, angular face. "You have seen your truth?"

Elya couldn't quite get her spinning thoughts under control. "I…don't know." Except she did. All this time, she'd thought the Temple of Atonement would be the solution to all her problems. Instead, it had shown her what the solution was. "I have to go."

"Elya." Pomante stood as Elya did, heading for the gates without bothering to gather her things. "Elya," she called. "If you go, you can never return."

Weeks, days, even hours ago, that statement would have ripped her in two. Instead, hearing it now, knowing what she did, feeling what she felt, she smiled at Pontame. "I know."

"You and I need to have a discussion about digging." Gareth bent down in front of a mud-covered Tyrus and held the dead Jessaberry root in his hand. The pup had been digging up plants east and west. "This is bad for business. Leave them alone, you hear me?" Tyrus whimpered, ducked down, and pushed his head into Gareth's free hand. Gareth sighed, the irritation flowing out of him. "I know, little guy. I miss her, too."

His return to his land had been done in the blink of an eye, or more with a flick of his wrist. His time with Ijaro and the other Zentali had shown him his denying his magic was causing more pain than acknowledging it. It was time to be who and what he was, no hesitation. No regrets.

It would start with him. People would just have to get used to the idea a Zentali was living in the Forgotten Realm. And once they got used to him, they could get used to all the others. It would take time, but it seemed time was all he had.

"I see you've found a helper."

Anger spurted but didn't quite surge at the sound of his mother's voice. "I thought we agreed you'd leave me alone?" He turned as he stood and found her behind him, wearing one of her gowns, not white this time, but a deep turquoise trimmed with silver. "What do you want, Callandra?"

"Just some time. And perhaps some conversation. Have you any of that wine left?"

Was it his imagination or was she nervous? "Sure. Why don't you stay out here with Tyrus. I'll get you a glass."

"All right." She crouched and held out her hands to the montari, surprising Gareth with a laugh when Tyrus bounded over and almost knocked her to the ground. When he returned with two glasses, he assumed she'd drink, say her peace and be gone. Instead, she walked over to the porch and took a seat in the solitary chair. "It's been brought to my attention I've underestimated you, Gareth. In your ability to protect yourself and to accept the truth."

"What truth? Yours?"

"I'd appreciate at least the appearance of civility, Gareth. Please." Temper flashed in her eyes, but again, she appeared to rein herself in. "What happened between your father and me—"

"Was a long time ago. I get it. Don't worry. If that's why you came here, you can leave now."

"You get what, exactly?"

"It's difficult to be a mother to a child you're ashamed of."

"Ashamed?" Callandra gasped. "What makes you think—"

"I'm Zentali. My father—"

"Your father was the only man I've ever truly loved." Callandra cut him off, then took a long drink of wine. "She was right. I've failed you in so many ways."

"Who was right?"

"Elya."

His heart leaped at the mere mention of her name. "What does Elya—"

"It was my mistake, my ignorant prejudices and fears that stoked the hatred of the Zentali. What happened to you and your father's people was wrong, and I will do everything I can, moving forward, to remedy that. I was too easily influenced by council members who could only see their own interests and Jartho saw that before I did. And he knew something had to be done to protect you."

"Protect me?"

"If it had been known I had a Zentali son, the Realms would have devolved into chaos. I was already struggling against Dracha and his efforts to get a foothold on my throne. Your father knew we had to send you away, with no way to find you. To protect you from Dracha. To protect you from my advisors. And my people."

Gareth froze. Something she'd said…. "No way to find me. What are you saying?"

Callandra folded her hands in her lap. "Your father confessed to treason to take the attention away from you, so you could be taken away and put in Ijaro's care. He drew out his confession, allowed them to torture him, to keep them focused on him. By the time they executed him—"

"You executed him." His stomach rolled until he thought he might be ill. "You're telling me my father sacrificed himself to protect me."

"Yes." Callandra held out her hands. "If you do not believe me, I can show you."

He shook his head even as it spun. It made sense. So much made sense now. "But why?"

She lowered her arms. "Because you were his son. And because he loved you more than anything in this world. Even me."

"But I'm only one person. He was the best of us. The most reasonable, rational. He could have saved our people had he not been—"

Callandra jumped to her feet, raced toward him so she could look out over the valley. "She's in trouble." She lifted her arms. The clouds raced past. The sky darkened before lightning cracked and split the ground in the distance.

"Who?"

"Elya. Why isn't she using her magic to get back?"

"Get back? Elya's coming back?"

At the sound of Elya's name, Tyrus let out a bark and began hopping about.

"Quiet the creature," Callandra ordered. "I need to concentrate." She stretched her palms up, brought them down in a fast circle and set a portal to spinning beside the ramshackle house. The portal twisted and turned. Callandra's face shifted and finally, she wrenched her arms back and Elya dropped through the spinning air. She landed hard and Gareth heard the breath whoosh out of her.

Callandra stumbled back and shook Gareth off. "See to her."

Gareth ran for Elya as she pushed herself up. Her clothes—a tangle of skirts and fabric, were ripped and covered in dirt. Her face was smudged, her hair, her once beautiful long hair, now a debris field of leaves and twigs. "I got lost." She spit out dirt and frowned. "All those paths we took to the Temple disappeared once I got there. Funny no one told me that." She glared at the goddess so vehemently Gareth fell in love with her all over again.

He bent down and hauled her into his arms. "You left. You left the temple."

"I did." Her voice was muffled against his chest.

"You can't go back." Why was he arguing? Why did he care? "Elya, how—"

"Someone made me realize just how much I do love you. No illusion. No spell." She leaned back and grinned up at him. "Just love."

He kissed her. Kissed her the way he'd been dreaming about. Kissed her the way he had the first time and every time since.

"You could have offered to bring me with you," Elya grumbled when Gareth led her to where Callandra and Tyrus waited for them. The pup leapt up into her arms and began licking the dirt from her face.

"I could have," Callandra said. "Consider that penance for your attitude."

"Attitude? Elya?" Gareth asked with feigned shock.

"Have you worked everything out?" Elya looked to Callandra for the answer.

"Nearly. There is still much atonement to be done. For the damage I caused to the Zentali." Callandra blinked tears away. "It is my greatest shame that my hatred and distrust led to so many deaths. Oh, Elya. You're beautiful hair." She reached out and brushed a ragged strand from her face. "What happened?"

"You don't know?" Gareth asked.

"No," Elya told him. "She doesn't. Because she can't see anything when it comes to the Zentali."

"Elya, please. I'm trying to make amends—" Callandra frowned.

"That's not what I mean. You can't see anything when it comes to the Zentali because of Gareth. In the vision, something Jartho said."

"You saw my father?" Envy sliced through him.

"I saw him and your mother together. Gareth, when he left you, did he give you something? Leave you with anything?"

"Only this." He lifted his hand, indicated the tattoo encircling his wrist.

"Jartho said he'd taken precautions to protect his people. You, Gareth. You were his last gift to your people. You're a shield. As long as you live, the Zentali remain safe in hiding. Or at least safe from those wishing them harm."

"Elya," Gareth snapped, astonished she'd reveal his people's secrets.

"It's all right. Your mother's come around, haven't you, Callandra? Your animosity against the Zentali has faded, has it not? Given the chance, you'd do what you could to make it up to them?"

"If that were only possible. Because of me, only Gareth and a few others—"

"She doesn't know." Gareth whispered, unable to tear his gaze from his mother's face. She had no idea how many Zentali lived. "I've always been able to tell when you were lying, and you aren't. Not about this."

"I don't know what?"

"The Zentali survived, Callandra," Elya said. "They've survived and thrived and evolved. And if you'll agree to lifting the banishment, if you'll agree to give them a place to live, out in the open, and lift your decree against them, Gareth can bring them here. You can begin to earn their forgiveness."

"Here?" Gareth turned his head, and over Elya's head, where the endless valley he'd fallen in love with ages ago sat, he could see what she did. Feel what she did. "I can bring them here?"

"It would be a chance to prove I am worthy of your love," Callandra whispered. "A chance to get to know my son and earn his forgiveness as well." She nodded. "Yes. Bring them. I will do as you ask, Elya. And I will do one more thing." She stepped close and placed her hands on either side of Elya's face.

Gareth closed his eyes against the flash of light. When he could see again, he saw Elya, in her traveling clothes, her long, silver hair braided down her back. And when she lifted the hand not holding Tyrus, a flame burst to life.

"My magic," Elya whispered. "I have my magic back."

"It is the least I can do. Now." Callandra smoothed a hand down the front of her gown. "I am ready to meet your people, Gareth."

"I don't know how…."

Elya folded her hand into his and the warmth of her, the magic of her, pulsed through him. He looked down as the markings around his wrist vanished.

Callandra gasped. Elya turned and as Gareth returned his gaze to the valley, he saw every dwelling, every person, every stall, creature, and torch appear. He had pulled the entirety of his people, Larius and his family included, to the place he had made his home. The cries and startled shouts erupted and echoed toward them. And there, Gareth saw, with her bright silver hair, held high in her father's arms, Isa lifted her hands to the bright, open sky and laughed.

"Thank you," Gareth choked, as the bands that had been locked around his heart dropped away. He looked at Callandra and moved forward to draw Elya into his arms. "Thank you, Mother."

"I see many things," Elya said as the Zentali headed their way, dozens upon dozens, racing forward. "I see a beginning. I see hope. I see love. And it's all perfect." She looked over her shoulder and leaned into his arms. "Simply perfect."

Copyright © 2019 by Anna J. Stewart.

After receiving her MBA from Cornell University, Tonya D. Price worked for over fifteen years as an executive in the internet industry and at universities before becoming a full-time writer. She has published numerous short stories in magazines and anthologies. Her thriller short story "Payback," first published in Fiction River's Hard Choices, *will appear in* The Best Mystery Stories of 2019. *Tonya also writes the non-fiction series,* Business Books for Writers. *You can follow Tonya at: www.TonyaDPrice.com or connect with her on twitter @TonyaDPrice2.*

UNDER A SOLSTICE MOON

by Tonya D. Price

Ava burst into the ferry's galley kitchen. She ran smack into a skinny teenage waiter balancing a round tray of sizzling Keftedes meatballs above his shaven head. Ground beef patties flew through the air. The boy stood as if dazed for a moment before lunging at her. She side-stepped him, one sneaker sliding on a piece of lettuce, taking her just out of his reach. Catching herself prevented her falling flat on her face, but her left knee paid the price. She regained her footing, the knee aching as she dodged a thrown banana.

The chorus of curses from the kitchen crew drowned out the groans of an overhead air conditioner. Drenched in sweat from the blistering temperatures radiating from two giant stoves, Ava risked a quick glance over her left shoulder. She expected the Albanian to burst through the galley door at any moment.

No sign of him.

Yet.

She shoulder-slammed the side exit door and darted into a throng of summer tourists lining up to depart the ship. Fresh ocean air cleared her throbbing head, but the relief didn't last. Three ear-splitting blasts from the ship's horn announced their arrival into Paros Bay.

A hell of a way for an archeologist to arrive at a dig.

Not that she was an archeologist.

Dad would be furious if he were alive. But then this whole mess was his fault.

Ava adjusted her black LL Bean backpack on her tired shoulders. She debated her next move. Her chances of actually getting off the ship without being retained dwindled by the minute.

Above the engine drone she heard a high-pitched voice call, "Ava! Ava Pappas!"

The Albanian. She couldn't see him in the crowd, but she knew the voice only too well. Two older Greek widows wearing traditional black dresses blocked her path. She pushed her way past them with a quick "Excuse me," using her rusty Greek. Putting more room between herself and the Albanian, Ava ducked under the arm of a man wearing a sweatshirt featuring a photo of the Acropolis. He called out a favorite American obscenity as she squeezed past a girl taking a selfie.

"Hey! What's your hurry," demanded a deep male voice in English wrapped in a Greek accent. Strong fingers dug into her arm, pulling her to an abrupt stop. "We will all get off the boat in due time."

A sudden twist to the left, then right, didn't free her. The stranger only tightened his grip. Lunging backward didn't work either. Rather than escape, her struggle resulted in her captor grabbing her by both shoulders and pulling her to his chest. Peering over his muscled bare arms, she watched the Albanian, no more than fifteen feet away, stop his pursuit. Biding his time. Apparently, he didn't want to confront her in public. Good to know.

Three more blasts from the horn signaled the porters to open the exit gate, allowing passengers to proceed in an orderly walk down the ferry's off ramp.

"Ava? Is that you?" The stranger pushed her back, extended his arms. For the first time she got a good look at his face. The kind of face you couldn't help staring at. Not with those blue eyes. Ava forgot the Albanian and the trauma at the airport.

The man holding her wore a black t-shirt and jeans. Sneakers too clean to belong to a sailor. Something about those eyes seemed familiar. And then she made the connection. "Nickolas?" After twenty years, she couldn't be certain this was her Nickolas until that old familiar smile spread in delight.

"Ava." He pulled her into a tight bear hug. "I can't believe it's you."

Could this be the boy she had loved twenty years ago?

Thank goodness he seemed happy to see her. There had been bad feelings when she left.

That came with breaking someone's heart.

He still wore his Greek fisherman hat tilted to one side because as he told her once, it made him look like Kostas Sommers. At sixteen, she recognized the similarities, a little bit. At thirty-six Nickolas could be the famous Greek movie star's twin. Except for those eyes the color of the blue Aegean sky. Nickolas had the brown-eyed Kostas beat on that account.

Despite her instinct to run, Ava held off and instead checked for her pursuer. The Albanian had slipped into the crowd.

He excelled at disappearing.

She forced herself to concentrate on an escape plan as she and Nickolas shuffled forward with the line of departing passengers inching toward the ramp. For the moment, Nickolas' presence seemed to keep the Albanian at bay, so she walked alongside him as if they were the couple they once had been.

As Nickolas talked of his parents, Ava tried to plot her next move in case the Albanian reappeared. At the bottom of the ramp, she could see a mass of people. Locals colliding with a German tour group wearing matching purple T-shirts. Agios Yanis, the Summer Solstice Festival, drew visitors from around the world.

"Did you?"

Nickolas' question pulled her back from her woolgathering. What was he asking? He looked so concerned and for a moment, her mind went blank. It wasn't just his beautiful face, although with his olive complexion and jet-black hair and perfect features he could make her forget everything with just the hint of a smile. Once he had been her entire universe. Could this have been her father's secret plan? To force her to return to Paros in hopes she would meet Nickolas again on the most romantic night of the year?

She tried to hide her confusion with a smile. "I'm sorry. I'm afraid I am tired from the trip. Did I what?"

Nickolas frowned. "What's wrong?"

The question caught her off-guard, and she blurted out the truth or the part she could tell. "I don't know. A man started following me at the Athens airport. He's on the ferry. Every time I look around, I see him. I don't know what he wants." Her honesty confused her. She was already thinking of him as a friend. He wasn't her friend, she reminded herself. Just an old boyfriend who broke up with her when she needed a friend the most.

Nickolas surveyed the crowd behind them. "Do you see him now?"

She shook her head in reply. "No. He vanished when I ran into you."

They had reached the bottom of the ramp and fought through the crush of the mob. Frustrated passengers, tired from the four-hour ferry ride, attempted to push their way through a battalion of local men who earned their living by receiving a bounty for every tourist they brought to the hotels. Strolling holiday visitors, oblivious to the confrontation unwittingly joined the fray.

The hectic scene, always stressful, proved more so during festival times. Vendors eager to make as much money as possible off the tourists, blocked the wide pier in an effort to sell their plastic wreaths and bundles of dry flowers.

"Let's find a place to talk." Nickolas took her hand and led her through the chaotic mass of people. Women stepped backward to let him pass. Men did the same. A few of the local guys looked as if they wanted to challenge him, but they stepped out of his way. People just naturally tried to please Nickolas. Oblivious to his charisma, Nickolas never seemed to understand the power his physical attractiveness had on those around him. That was his charm.

Once they broke free of the shoulder to shoulder crowd, they emerged on the main street that ran through coastal town of Parikia. They turned down one of the oldest streets in the village. Villagers outlined each stone in the pavement in white paint to match the white walls of the houses—a hallmark of the island.

Nickolas guided Ava a short distance before pointing toward two outdoor café chairs in front of a bakery. "Let's sit and catch up. I can't believe you are back on Paros."

She stopped, ever on the lookout for the Albanian. "Maybe we could sit inside?"

"If it would make you more comfortable."

The café aromas brought back old memories of happier times. She took a minute to inhale the intoxicating whisp of strong Greek coffee, freshly baked pastries and a variety of honeyed baklava. Once she had danced to the traditional Greek music playing from a sound system. A group of gray-bearded men sat in a line of five chairs by open windows smoking unfiltered cigarettes. They nodded a greeting at Nickolas as he entered. The villagers all knew each other.

She hoped they didn't remember her.

Ava hesitated, but Nickolas just waved at the young woman behind the counter. Speaking Greek, he asked, "Are there seats free below?"

"Yes, yes." The girl said, tucking a strand of purple dyed hair behind one ear. "Of course."

They ordered two Greek coffees and descended the narrow stairway to the basement. If the Albanian were to appear, Ava didn't see a way to escape. Maybe she would have been safer on the veranda after all.

They sat opposite of each other in two wooden chairs at the far end of the tiny room. Ava chose the chair closest to the stairs. She tried to relax. "So, Nickolas, what do you do?"

"Ah," he straightened in his chair, holding his head a bit higher than before. "I am a police officer. Ten years now."

Now Ava understood why people stepped out of Nickolas' way. And it made sense. He had always been one to follow the rules.

"I entered the academy after my mandatory military service. I am now a deputy." Nickolas leaned close. "Ava, we have more crime here than before." He paused for a minute. "Tell me the truth, you have no idea why this man is following you?"

Was he taking a personal interest or a professional interest?

She didn't know why the man followed her. She had told no one of her father's plan. "I flew from Boston to Athens, then got on the first ferry of the day. I have been traveling for," she counted in her head, "thirteen hours and I haven't slept for twenty-five."

Nickolas reached out and brushed a lock of her black hair off her face, the side of his hand lingering against her cheek. "You look exhausted but as beautiful as ever." For several minutes he said nothing, but he continued to watch her until she felt uncomfortable under his scrutiny. He broke the silence. "Tell me, what *do* you know of the man trailing you?"

"I first spotted him when I came out of the airport. He was watching me so intently he seemed to be waiting for me but," Ava hesitated, "I have

never seen him before. When I got a taxi to the ferry landing at Piraeus, I spotted him on the pier and thought he had followed me. I tried to put the whole thing down to coincidence, then on the ship, I heard someone call my name. I turned around, and he grabbed my wrist.

"I jerked my hand free and ran. Several times I saw him trailing me on the deck, but I managed to stay ahead of him. When I ran into you, he was behind us but then he …wasn't."

Nickolas began to drum his fingers on the table top. A nervous habit he retained from his youth. "I wouldn't worry. Men like this Albanian are cowards. He was probably looking for an easy mark. Most likely he has moved on to target someone else. My guess is he was also planning on traveling to Paros for the festival. Finding you on the ferry was probably just luck on his part."

"Maybe."

Nickolas sipped his coffee. "Why did you call him the Albanian?"

Ava shrugged. "Because he has a tattoo of the Albanian flag on the top of his right hand."

Nickolas looked down at the table. He didn't raise his head as if unable to look her in the eye when he said, "The Albanian drug gangs in Athens are well known. He wouldn't have any reason to think you might have any…."

She stood in anger, pushing her chair back so hard it tipped over. "I learned my lesson, Nico."

Embarrassed and ashamed by the reminder of her arrest and the pain she had caused her father, she ran up the stairs and out the door. Behind her Nickolas called her name, but she didn't slow down.

She kept running, even though she knew she couldn't outrun her past.

Twenty years ago, Nickolas had tried to warn her to not to go to the end of the year school party on the beach. She ignored him, putting down his insistence she stay home to mere jealousy.

She hadn't believed his claims there would be drugs at the party, but when the police rounded up everyone, one boy had a bag of weed. She was arrested with the boy although the police dropped the charges against her. Most of the parents blamed the deviant influence of the American girl for the appearance of drugs on the island.

Nickolas broke up with her. At the time, losing Nickolas seemed much worse than the prospect of jail time.

Coming back to Paros had been a mistake. At home in Boston, she thought she had put this all behind her and here she was having to relive the worst time of her life again. If she were to be caught tomorrow morning, she would have no one to turn to this time. At sixteen, the police might cut you some slack and order you off the island. At thirty-six they would not be so generous. Surely, her father must have known that when he wrote his will.

Her father's instructions said to stay at the Hotel Athena. The same hotel where she and her father had rented three modest rooms during his sabbatical year on the island.

When she reached the hotel, she hesitated before going inside, gathering her courage to face Mrs. Collias. However, afraid the Albanian might reappear, she forced herself to enter through the double doors. She didn't have a reservation. With so many tourists on the island they would have no rooms. And yet, her father wrote she was to arrive unannounced.

In the foyer the aroma of fresh cut wildflowers of all different colors greeted her, bringing back memories. Neatly displayed in a row on a simple wooden table sat three beautiful wreaths of dried flowers. Ava knew these were the Mayflower wreaths that every family made each year to celebrate the beginning of spring. Once she too had made such a wreath. Tomorrow these wreaths would be burned to launch the start of the summer solstice ceremony. Villagers would jump over the flames and make secret wishes, which tradition promised, would be granted by the fire magic.

Traditions weren't always right.

Ava rang a small brass bell shaped like Athena. Mrs. Collias appeared from a side door, wiping her hands dry on a dish cloth. She clapped her hands when she caught sight of Ava. She had taught Ava Greek in her kitchen during the cooking and afterwards during the dishwashing. She had helped Ava with her schoolwork and made the year after her real mother's death bearable.

On the same table where the flowers now sat, Mrs. Collias once showed Ava where to place her silent water and told her the legend, predicting that night she would dream of her future husband.

Most of what she had told Ava had been true.

"Ava, my girl. You have come back to us." The matronly hotel owner threw her arms around Ava. She had gained weight and her black hair had greyed, but her voice was the same. Kind and gentle. "It has been so long. Is your father with you?"

Sometimes Ava felt like all she had done for the past three weeks was retell and relive her father's death. Hard as it was, she broke the news to the one woman who had consoled her after the rest of the village shunned her.

Mrs. Collias sat down on a nearby settee, its blue and white checkered pattern long faded. She patted the spot beside her as she broke into tears at the news, then dried her face. "I am so glad to see you. I had always hoped you and your father might one day return. Have you seen his wall? It is a tourist site now. Can you imagine? People from all over Greece come to see the ancient wall."

Mrs. Collias attempted to relate in rapid fire Greek twenty years of village gossip in five minutes. She spoke so fast Ava had to ask her to slow down. "After all," she reminded the older woman, "I haven't spoken Greek in twenty years."

"Ah, but you remember so much. I can't tell Greek is not your mother tongue!"

"You are too kind. I can hear my American accent!" At one time she could go into Athens and pass for a Greek from the islands. Those days were gone.

"Stay a year with me, and your Greek will be good as new. Come, help in the kitchen. I'll have a girl prepare your room."

For the next hour Mrs. Collias' children started appearing in the doorway, news of their visitor's arrival traveling through the family. Throughout an impromptu meal of lamb Souvlaki finished off with Greek coffee and a delicious milk pie, Ava answered questions about her father's career and his passing.

The hotel was booked but Mrs. Collias had surprised Ava by giving her the same room she lived in before. Ava unpacked her suitcase, putting her clothes in a hand-carved stone dresser made of marble from the Paros' pit. Then, she removed her father's ancient Greek red stone pot, sealed with a special bonding agent according to her father's directions. She still couldn't believe airport security let her through with the vessel after a brief inspection.

She placed the pot on a small round table in front of the double French door to the veranda. Once she loved the veranda and the freedom it gave her to come and go as she wished. Now she worried the Albanian could easily break in through the thin glass and old lock. "Okay, Dad. Do something useful. Warn me if the Albanian tries to get in."

Jet lag and a time difference of seven hours, combined to wake Ava at five in the morning, an hour before dawn on the longest day of the year. No fancy dresses for this hike. She pulled on a pair of old blue jeans and a dark pullover, not at all her typical attire. No need to draw attention to herself this morning. If someone couldn't tell if she were a man or a woman, so much the better.

Many of the island's population held small farms and farmers rose at dawn to care for their animals. Therefore, Ava had to carry out her father's wishes in the dark, like the criminal she was about to become. For several minutes she stared at her backpack debating whether to refuse her father's request. Who did she owe the greater loyalty? Mrs. Collias or her father? Stupid question. No matter the consequences she would grant her father his last wish. Besides, with luck, no one would ever discover her crime.

She slipped out the hotel door. Thousands of stars twinkled above her, the waxing moon having set. Tomorrow the full solstice moon would fill the sky with light all night long. Once on the beach she had lain in Nickolas arms beneath such a moon, listening to his stories of star-crossed lovers and their ancient tales.

In the harbor the horns of outgoing fishing boats could be heard. She took their calls as a warning to hurry.

She cut through the side and back streets until she reached the steep dry creek bed that ran between the island's lone mountain summit down to the port of Parikia. For every step she took, her foot slipped on the pebbles making the climbing hard. Twice she stumbled in the dark. Once she cut her hand on a sharp rock, but she kept hiking until she reached the first pasture. A lone bird high above in a tree, startled perhaps by her footsteps, sang a warning.

She kept climbing. Fifteen minutes later, tired and still feeling the effects of her cross-Atlantic trip, she reached the ancient wall her father had marked on a hand drawn map. As a protected site, no one could disturb the ground. To do so and get caught would result in imprisonment. The Greeks, with good reason, had harsh penalties for disturbing their antiquities. Her father must have known the risk and yet being buried here meant so much to him he had created this elaborate plan.

Ava would have traveled to this spot even if her father hadn't made the trip a condition of his will. All he had to do was ask. Why hadn't he just asked?

What did it matter? She was here. Airport security hadn't confiscated dear old dad, and now all she had to do was break Greek law and give him a final resting place.

Maybe tonight, she would jump the flames, ask the Greek gods to cleanse her of her sins. Perhaps she might even bring silent water back with her again and in a few days return to Boston to resume her life.

Her lonely and solitary life.

She lowered her backpack to the ground, took out her collapsible archeological shovel and began to dig. With the hole the depth and width her father requested she reached into her backpack and pulled out the stone jar. Ava lowered the pot into the hole.

"Hands up!"

Lights came on from all directions blinding Ava. Out of the white haze, the Albanian rushed her, grabbing her arm and jerking her wrists behind her back before she could react. "I am a Captain Gashi of the Greek Drug Enforcement Agency."

She felt steel handcuffs snap on her wrists. "Ava Pappas, you are under arrest for transporting drugs into Greece from the United States."

A police officer pulled the stone vase out of the ground and pulled out a knife to try and pry off the lid.

"Wait, wait." She cried out, " Those are my father's ashes, not drugs."

The officer had no luck with the knife. He lifted the pot over his head as if to smash the pot on the ground.

The Albanian raised his hand. "Just a minute."

The police officer hesitated, then lowered the pot.

The Albanian spun Ava around by the arms to face him. "Your father's ashes?"

"Yes, yes. My father's last request was he be buried beside the ancient wall he discovered."

The policeman shook the pot next to his ear. "Sounds like powder inside."

"No," Ava insisted, "it sounds like ashes. My father's ashes. He requested I bury him next to this wall on the morning of the summer solstice."

The Albanian studied her for a moment. "Why the summer solstice?"

Ava told the truth. "I have no idea. He was an archeologist. He probably read in some old book to do so would bring luck to mankind. I really don't know. He is—was—the only living family I had and so," she shrugged. "I am doing what he asked." Then, just to be completely honest, she added, "and he put in his will I wouldn't inherit anything unless I followed his instructions." As an afterthought, she added, "I brought a copy of his will. It's in my backpack."

The Albanian sighed and jerked his head to one side in a signal for another agent to search the backpack. After fishing around inside the man produced the document. The Albanian read for a few minutes. "The request is in the will." He folded the will in half. "We will need to verify that ashes are in the pot, but, if you are telling the truth, we will return your father's ashes to you." He took the handcuff key from his pocket and freed her.

"Wait!" The local village policeman held a hand over his eyes. "Cut those damn lights."

The lights went out. On the horizon, the sun started to peak out over a calm ocean, casting enough light to see.

"Disturbing an antiquity site is against the law," the officer pointed out. "If you don't arrest her, I will."

"That is true." Nickolas, buttoning up his police jacket, stepped into view. "Except, this is not the ancient wall," he told the officer. "This is the foundation of an old stone goat fence my father put in twenty-three years ago with Dr. Pappas' help. Up there," he pointed further up the mountain, "Is the ancient wall."

The policeman, determined to make an arrest, tried again. "Then she trespassed on your property."

Nickolas looked at Ava, not his colleague as he spoke. "The daughter of Dr. Pappas always has my permission to dig on my family's land any time she pleases."

The two policemen began arguing in Greek, while the Albanian gave Ava a stern warning. "I believe these are your father's remains but don't leave Paros until we confirm the contents of the pot."

"I won't."

The Albanian drove Ava back to the Athens Hotel. When she entered the foyer, she found the hotel staff bustling around preparing the breakfast room for early rising guests. Ava nodded her greetings and made her way to her room and went to sleep.

Greek music from the street outside her veranda woke her up six hours later, followed by a knock at the door.

"Ava! Get up! It is time to take the wreaths to the town square!" Mrs. Collias opened the creaking wood door to peek in. Without an invitation, she entered to leave a plate of sweet almond pastries and Greek coffee on the small table where Ava had left her father to stand watch over her the night before. "I hear you went for an early morning walk."

Once again Ava had broken the poor women's trust. "I'm sorry. I couldn't tell anyone…."

Mrs. Collias laughed and waved off Ava's confession. "I wonder what your father would think if he knew that you could not even find his wall!".

The older woman closed the door before Ava could answer.

Ava groaned. News travelled fast. Especially embarrassing news

Well, it had been twenty years.

And it was dark.

And she was sure she had followed her father's directions just as he wrote them….

At the square the unmarried Collias daughters placed their flower wreaths on the cobblestones several feet apart. Throughout the huge square, the local families had done the same.

As dusk arrived, several politicians gave speeches while the tourists took pictures and girls practiced jumping over the wreaths. The square came alive with tourists and locals mixing as if old friends. When the sun dipped below the ocean, the church bells rang.

The patriarchs of the families stepped forward and with great ceremony lit the wreaths with long matches. Children, teenagers, men and even some women took turns jumping over the burning flowers until small piles of orange embers remained scattered throughout the square.

With the last of the fires out, a group of village girls and women lined up at the ancient stone well in the middle of the square. Each carried a bronze pitcher to fill with water. The boys teased them and made funny faces trying to get them to talk. If the boys succeeded, the girls were required to empty their jars and refill them from the well. They must remain mute until they brought what the legend called, "the silent water," home.

A group of women Ava had known from school came up to hug her and greet her. They insisted she meet their husbands and children. To Ava's amazement everyone seemed happy to see her. And of course, everyone laughed at the idea she had tried to bury her father beside a goat wall. Not one person mentioned the scandal of so long ago.

When the last of the fires went out people began to leave the square. "Ava. Can you forgive me?"

She looked behind her and saw Nickolas standing with his head down, his policeman's hat in his hands. He looked like a small boy afraid to face her.

"Forgive you? What for? Even I thought I was breaking the law by going to the wall."

He sighed and all the feelings she once had for him came back to her with such force she fought to keep her emotions in check.

Nickolas took a step away from her, putting distance between the two of them. "I have a confession. I know Captain Gashi quite well. Drugs have become a real problem on Paros among the island kids. When he called me to tell me that you were carrying a suspicious pot, I...." He looked away. "I considered the worst case scenario because of, you know, your past."

"You knew I was coming to Paros?"

He nodded. Still he did not look at her. "That was why I was on the ferry. To help Captain Gashi detain and interview you, but then, I *wanted* you to be innocent. We made a deal. If I were to find you first, I could talk to you, to see if, maybe, you had," he shrugged, "some other reason for returning."

Nickolas had planned to capture her? He thought she was bringing drugs to Paros? "I can understand Captain Gashi thinking I was transporting drugs, but you, Nickolas?"

"I am sorry."

He looked so miserable she found her anger hard to maintain.

She could never be mad at him. Always, even when they were younger, she couldn't stand to see him unhappy. She knew he meant well. "I can see why someone might think I was carrying drugs, especially after what was *thought* to have happened before. And in fact," she took a deep breath, "I was surprised they didn't seize the pot at the airport."

"Oh, security noticed, but they decided to let you through in hopes of capturing the person you were selling to."

"Why did you let me go when I ran away at the café?"

Nickolas shifted from one foot to another. "I didn't—not exactly. You are quite difficult to catch, you know."

That was the first lie Nickolas had ever told her, but she didn't give away she knew. "Sorry to disappoint you."

Nickolas looked up and smiled. "You have never disappointed me."

"Except once."

"You were young. We both were. I never forgave myself for not going with you to that party."

"Why?" She never suspected he might have felt guilty over what had happened. "You were right to refuse to go. I should have listened to you."

"I should have protected you."

"No, I should have protected myself and been smarter. My father refused to let me to go, and I went to the party anyway. You were both right. Besides, if you had gone with me, you might not have been able to become a policeman and I imagine you are a very good one."

Nickolas surveyed the remaining people in the square. "I'm not sure if you are making fun of me or not."

"No, I'm very impressed, Nickolas. And I owe you a lot for standing up for me today."

A group of maintenance men began sweeping the square, collecting the ashes of the wreaths. They waved at Nickolas but kept their distance.

He waved back, then returned his attention to Ava. "I knew your father well enough to know that he would have made such a request of you. But I'm afraid this is one plan of your father's that will not come to pass. No one wants his remains buried at the ancient wall."

Ava feared her family had lost the trust of the villagers yet again. "He never meant to insult anyone. He loved this town."

Nickolas took her hand and led her to a nearby bench. They sat down side by side. "And they loved him. Everyone feels honored he thought so much of this village that he wanted his burial here. They are insisting he be laid to rest at the entrance to the ancient cemetery. They are even raising money for his gravestone."

Ava knew how much her father would appreciate such a gesture. "He would be so honored."

"I think his plan did come together, you know," Nickolas flashed that grin she couldn't resist. "Marking the goat wall as the ancient wall was a stroke of genius, if his goal was to bring us back together. He would never ask you to commit a crime."

"He could have told me! I'm sorry I didn't tell you ahead of time what I was doing. But he made me promise to keep the whole thing a secret."

Nickolas sighed. "I understand. You should know something though: Over the years, people came to realize that you had nothing to do with the drugs at the party. Your arrest came from overzealous officers and one boy's stupidity. No one blames you anymore for what happened."

Ava leaned her head against his shoulder. "Thank you. For telling me. I was so afraid they all still hated me."

After several minutes of silence, Nickolas stroked her hair.

"Ava," his warm breath and deep baritone sent a shiver through her as he spoke into her ear. "Do you remember when we went down to German beach after the Festival of Agios Yanis?"

She remembered. "You mean when we went skinny dipping in the moonlight?"

"I mean when we made love for the first time on the beach under the solstice moon."

Her breathing quickened to match his. "That was a long time ago."

He folded his arms around her. "They say the waters on this night cleanse you of your sins."

She laughed. "They say that jumping over the burning wreaths three times cleanse you of your sins.

I had already done that. *And* carried the silent water to Mrs. Collias' house."

"And did you dream of your future husband that night as the old legends say?" He didn't wait for an answer but kissed her as he had kissed her that night on the beach.

When she could speak, she admitted, "I dreamed of you, Nickolas. You have always been the man of my dreams."

"And you the woman of mine."

Ava had no doubt her father was watching from the heavens, crossing the stars above the two lovers.

Copyright © 2019 by Tonya D. Price.

Johanna Rothman writes about quirky smart women who aren't afraid to stand up for themselves. Her short stories have been in two volumes of Pulphouse, as well as You Really Liked That?, *and one volume of Fiction River. An award-winning non-fiction writer, Johanna has published fourteen books about management in all forms. Her most recent book is* From Chaos to Successful Distributed Agile Teams *with Mark Kilby. See her newsletter, articles, blogs, and more about her books at www. jrothman.com. She also writes personal essays at www.createadaptablelife.com*

QUEENIE'S RESCUE

by Johanna Rothman

As her shuttle bus pulled up to Bishop's Lodge, Joanie sighed—again—with the wonder of it all. The shuttle had met them at the Albuquerque airport. She swore the blue of the sky was lighter, crisper, and cleaner than back home in Boston. It was gorgeous. New Mexico really was the Land of Enchantment.

She'd been glued to the window the entire drive up from Albuquerque. They had climbed up to the mesa and had climbed even more in altitude to get to Santa Fe. She'd had to swallow to clear her ears several times. Although, she wondered if part of that clearing was the speed at which the driver climbed the hills.

She wasn't sure what she expected, but these rolling hills were nothing like the rolling hills of New England. Back home, you could sort of tell the horizon was only a few miles away. Here? She had no idea. The hills rose to a mesa and then you could see forever. They'd descended into Santa Fe a little, and then climbed again to the Bishop's Lodge.

The architecture was like nothing she'd ever seen, either. Everything was stucco or adobe, with the ever-present ladders on the outside of the buildings. She was pretty sure the log extensions from the buildings collected rain water, what there was of it.

Joanie felt lucky that she'd picked up a fresh water bottle in the airport. She'd steadily drunk it through the hour-plus drive. It was almost done, and she was ready for another. Her mouth wasn't uncomfortably dry, but she sure did notice it.

Her stomach gurgled. She'd been on the road since nine this morning, and she was ready for a good meal and then bed. Ah, maybe just bed.

As she stepped out of the van, she sneezed. Their Vermont location had a "perfume," as they liked to call it, of wild flowers and manure, emphasis on the manure. Here? Just the manure with a hint of sage.

She looked around for the animals. They were down the small hill on the other side of the driveway.

She looked again. Driveway was too tame a word. This was a boulevard, wide enough for at least three cars across. She stood on pavement. The drive wound in a small S, down near the horses, some kind of hard-packed rust-colored dirt.

She sneezed again, thinking it was time to get more water.

"Ma'am?" said a deep voice.

Joanie turned around. Oh my. If this wasn't a definition of tall, dark, and handsome, she didn't know what was.

She couldn't quite see his eyes because he had on mirrored sunglasses underneath a huge black cowboy hat. He wore a light blue t-shirt that showed off his arms and his chest, as well as faded denim jeans. He looked scrumptious. She was already looking forward to the other view.

"Ma'am?" he asked again.

"Oh, yes!" Joanie said, as a flush rose up her neck. "Sorry, I didn't realize you were talking to me."

His left cheek had a dimple that she swore winked at her.

"Yes, ma'am," he said. "Would you like some more water?"

"Thanks, I would," she said.

He extended his hand, holding a bottle of water.

As she took it, she swore she felt electricity spring up her arm. She shivered.

He smiled again, this time more broadly. "Well, ma'am," he said. "I think we have some chemistry. Or, maybe some electricity."

Joanie smiled. Chemistry with him might be lovely. "Thanks," she said.

"I'm Jesse," he said.

"I'm Joanie," she said.

He extended his hand. She took it.

The two of them were stuck until the cowboy next to him nudged Jesse hard enough that he had to take a step sideways. Jesse finally released her hand.

The other cowboy said, "I'm Bart, nice to meet you."

Joanie thought Bart was certainly tall and cute, but not like Jesse. "Nice to meet you, too."

"Welcome to Bishop's Lodge," Jesse said. "Maybe you'll come on a horse ride later this week."

Joanie frowned. "Well, I'm not so sure of that. First, I have work."

"Work," he said, "On a dude ranch?" Jesse paused. "You're from back East, right?"

Joanie nodded.

"Let me give you a piece of advice," he said. "Leave the work in your room and come out and play. You won't regret it."

Joanie wasn't so sure about the not regretting, but she sure did want to come out and play with him.

"My boss is coming out in a couple of days," she said. "I need to get everything ready by then. And, we'll be busy all week." She paused. "And, I'm afraid of horses."

Jesse frowned. "Afraid of horses?" he asked.

She nodded.

He leaned over and whispered. "I have a secret for you."

"What?" she whispered back.

"We have horses here." There was a beat of silence. He grinned.

She laughed. "I *do* know that," she said. "But, thank you."

He nodded. "Miss Joanie, what do you do?"

"I'm an event planner," she said. "We'll be working with management to help market the Lodge for offsites and weddings."

Jesse took her hand in his, again. "Well then, Miss Joanie," he said, as he shook it slowly, "I'll just have to entice you to come out and play."

This time his dimple winked on and stayed on. Oh, he was a charmer all right.

Joanie sneezed again. Jesse motioned to the water.

She opened the water and took a big gulp. Oh, so much better to have something cool and clean go down her throat. "Thanks."

She walked up the three steps to the lodge and turned around. Jesse was still watching her. He touched two of his fingers to his hat and gave a little bow.

Joanie was still walking on air when she reached the reception desk inside the lodge. She might need to give herself a little talking-to, if she was going to get any work done this week.

Joanie awakened at six, to the sun streaming into her room. Between the travel and the altitude last night, she hadn't taken enough notice of her room. Now, she really looked to see how nice the her accommodation was. She could use this information when she spoke with clients.

The decadent king-size bed had been very comfortable. Even the pillows were comfy. Too often, hotel pillows were like rocks. Not these. She walked over to the beehive fireplace. She'd heard those fireplaces were called kivas. She'd have to check that out. She sat in first the right and then the left of the two brown upholstered chairs on either side of the fireplace. Oh, comfy. Very nice touch.

She sneezed a couple more times as she got dressed for breakfast. She might have to get some kind of an antihistamine. She wondered what she was allergic to.

She got dressed and realized how thirsty she was. She drained last night's plastic water bottle, the one from Jesse. She grabbed her sunglasses and her steel water bottle that went with her on every trip. She left her room, headed for the dining room just past the registration desk.

At first glance, the dining room looked like a cross between what she expected of a dude ranch and a high-end dining room. The high-backed chairs, upholstered with brown leather, each had arms. She could see wooden legs underneath the snow-white tablecloths. The crystal looked real. This would be a great place for a wedding, never mind high-end corporate functions.

As she stood at the entrance, she turned to her right. Jesse was approaching, his long legs making just walking look like a graceful dance. His sunglasses were pushed up on top of his head, his hat in his right hand.

"Ready for breakfast?" he asked.

"I am!" she said. "Beyond ready, actually. I was too tired to really eat last night, so I'm starving."

"You've got to try the huevos rancheros," he said.

They sat down and the waitress, Dawn, came over to take her order. Joanie ordered the huevos rancheros and coffee.

Dawn asked, "Red, green, or Christmas?"

Joanie gave her a blank look. "What do you mean?"

Dawn smiled. "We ask what kind of chili—really like hot salsa—you want on your huevos," she said. "The heat level depends on the kind of pepper."

"I like spicy food," Joanie said. "But maybe I should ask which is mildest."

"The green is milder today," Dawn said. "But maybe you should try both. That would be Christmas."

"Okay," Joanie said. "Christmas it is." Research, if nothing else.

"What do you want to see today?" Jesse asked.

"Are you my guide?" Joanie asked, hoping.

Jesse grinned. "I sure am. I'm the general manager."

Joanie's face flushed. Of course. The general manager was a J. Goodman. Oh boy. How could she have forgotten?

"Your picture isn't anywhere on the literature you sent," she said.

Jesse laughed. "Would it have made a difference?"

"No," she said. "But I wouldn't feel like an idiot for not realizing you were the general manager."

Jesse leaned over and covered her hand and squeezed, just a little. "It's okay, Miss Joanie," he said. "You aren't an idiot. You're tired, hungry, and maybe just a little jet-lagged."

Joanie started to nod and sneezed instead. "I've got to get antihistamines today."

"Maybe not," he said. He reached into his shirt pocket and pulled out two bottles of saline nose spray. "I use the saline every day, because even though I've been here for years, the dryness still gets to me. Here's a new saline for you." He extended the unopened bottle to her.

Joanie looked at the spray bottle. "It looks like any other nose spray."

He grinned. "It's not. Just saline. You can use this forever and not mess up your nose. It might help your sneezing. Let me show you how to use it."

Jesse showed her how to take a big sniff in one nostril at a time. Joanie tried it. "Wow, I feel better already."

"Yup, your poor nose was all dried out."

Dawn returned with coffee for both of them. As they drank the coffee, Jesse told her about the Lodge, its history and the grounds. "I assume that the history might intrigue people, but the grounds will sell them?"

"That's what normally happens," she said.

To her surprise, she finished her entire breakfast, two cups of coffee and all. She felt great, ready to tackle the world.

"Did ya like it?" Jesse asked.

"Wonderful," she said. "You gotta love Christmas."

He grinned. "Let's start with the stables."

Joanie hesitated. "I have to tell you—"

"You're afraid of horses."

"Oh, yeah," she smiled shyly. "I told you last night."

"I'm not planning on curing you," he said. "But you need to get the feeling of the entire ranch if you're going to pitch it." He paused. "Our guests really like the horses."

He was right. She needed to see the stables and the horses.

As they left the lodge, they each put their sunglasses on. Jesse settled his hat firmly on his head.

They walked down to the stables, Joanie swinging her water bottle in her hand. Once they walked in, Joanie looking around her, surprised. "Ooh, I didn't expect this."

The stables were brightly lit, each stall cleaned. The stables smelled of hay, with just an overlay of manure. It didn't smell bad—it smelled earthy.

"This is so clean," Joanie said. "How do you keep it so clean?"

"We work at it," Jesse said with a little grin. "Our hands work hard to keep the stables clean. We assume our guests don't know that much about horses, so we work to make it easy for them to be here and learn." He paused. "And, if some of them want to curry the horses or shovel manure, we always say yes."

Joanie nodded.

Jesse leaned over and grabbed several carrot pieces out of the bag near the door. "Let's go to the ring and see how some of the horses are doing."

They walked into the sunshine and over to the corral.

Jesse held out a carrot to Joanie. "Here, put this on the flat part of your hand," he said. "You'll be able to make friends with one of the horses."

Joanie picked the carrot up by the end.

He grinned. "Nope, flat of your hand," he said. He picked up the carrot and ever so gently opened her hand. "Now, make your hand flat."

Joanie huffed. "Fine."

"It will be fine," he said gently, soothingly. "It will be just fine." Jesse whistled.

A huge horse ran over and stopped just in front of Jesse. Afraid, Joanie closed her hand around the carrot ready to bolt away from the large creature coming at her, but Jesse was faster.

Jesse's solid body kept hers firmly and confidently in place. He caught her hand in his and helped her open it again. "Hey, Queenie," he crooned. "Here's a lovely lady with a snack for you."

Joanie felt the softness of Queenie lips around the carrot and then it was gone.

"Wow!" she said. "That was fast!"

"And gentle?"

She smiled. "Yes, and gentle."

"And fun?"

Joanie thought. "Maybe fun. Maybe not. Fast."

"Do it again?"

"Nope. Not now."

"Still afraid?"

"Well, I need to practice with more carrots, but I'm not afraid of that."

"Excellent," he said. "First step, complete." He made a sign as if he was checking things off on a list. "On to the swimming pool, fitness center, and walking trails."

"Good thing I brought my supportive sneakers," Joanie said.

He looked at her shoes, and said, "We'll have to get you some boots for riding."

Joanie shook her head. "Nope, I'll skip the riding and the boots."

Jesse leaned forward and whispered in her ear, "You'd look unbelievable line-dancing in red Ariats. Let that sink into your head a little." He straightened.

Joanie flushed again. Well, that was a thought, wasn't it? Maybe she would do some shopping here.

They started to walk around the grounds.

After a couple of hours, Joanie was exhausted. She'd drunk all her water and then some. The Lodge had convenient mountain water spigots every so often on the trails. She'd refilled her water bottle, enjoying the sweet cool water every sip.

Now, her feet were tired, she was ready for lunch, and maybe a nap.

She had a quick lunch from the buffet. The iced tea was strong, the burritos filling, and the guacamole had a little kick. Time to relax first and then more observations. Or marketing copy.

Refreshed after her nap, Joanie started to write some of the sales copy she thought she'd use to sell the Lodge for events and weddings. She had a draft and thought she'd show it to Jesse before emailing it to her boss.

Her stomach growled, reminding her it was time to eat dinner.

She wandered over to registration, taking the long way around. The walkways were covered with arches with some sort of greenery twined around. It was as if she was in a world of her own. Romantic.

The day's heat was easing, but it was still quite dry and warm. She sneezed once and stopped walking. She pulled out her spray and sniffed one spray in each nostril. Better.

There were lights that looked a little like spaceships embedded in ground near the path, all pointed down.

She leaned over to look at one sign on top of the light. "Dark Sky Approved lighting. Please take a flashlight at night." Oh, maybe she could see stars tonight.

That would be a selling point, she thought. Oh, there was a lot here that were selling points.

She got to registration and saw Jesse waiting for her. He smiled, a big grin that showed both of his dimples. "Miss Joanie, did you have a nice relaxing afternoon?"

She smiled in return. "I did. I also had the time to work on some sales copy. Would you like to see it?"

"I would!" he said. "Come on into my office."

He led the way around the back of registration to a hallway she hadn't noticed before. The walls were a light gray, with several artist's rendering of the Lodge throughout the years.

She stopped at one, showing the Lodge at night, with sparkling lights on the grounds and lights in the night sky.

Jesse looked back at her, turned around and returned. "That's my favorite," he said in a hushed voice. "Every time I see that picture, I feel as if I'm part of the long history of Bishop's Lodge. We've changed the Lodge since then, at least every decade. But this picture, with the stars and the lights on the grounds—that picture helps me understand we're all part of this long line of hospitality and guests enjoying the New Mexico land."

Joanie nodded. "That's exactly how I feel."

They stood there a few seconds longer, looking at the picture together.

She broke the silence first. "Ready to review some sales copy?"

"Yup."

They walked into his office. It didn't look much like the offices she was accustomed to.

On the right was a long brown leather couch with end tables. Joanie wasn't sure what to call the furniture, except for "southwest." One wall was all small, narrow windows. No shades. She bet that the narrowness of the windows meant they didn't need shades to keep the sun out.

The wall behind his desk had trophies and ribbons.

Jesse saw her looking and gestured. "Back when I competed, I won a bunch."

"What made you decide to quit?" she asked.

"I was getting older, and realized I'd not just been lucky in my wins, but in not getting hurt. I still have all my teeth and all my ligaments. I decided to build a career where I could still enjoy myself riding and do something else that would be fun."

Joanie wrapped the loose string from her shirt hem around her finger.

He walked around his desk, piled high with papers. "Not so good with the paperwork though." He ducked his head a little to meet her gaze.

She laughed. "Do you have an admin?"

"Nope," he said. "Tried a few. They always created some kind of filing system I never really liked. I like mine."

She grinned. "I have the same problem."

The wall on the left had famous guests throughout the years at the lodge.

In the meantime, Jesse had taken her USB stick and printed the copy, one page for each of them.

She sat on the couch. He joined her, not too close, but close enough that she could smell the whiff of man, his scent. She liked it. A little earthy, a little bit of soap. Lots of Jesse.

They reviewed the sales copy. They went back and forth on some changes he wanted to make.

Finally, he said, "Look, you've got to come on a trail ride. Otherwise, you're missing a whole lot of what you could write about."

"Do you ever have a wagon follow you?"

"For multiple day rides," he said and grinned. "Want to sleep under the stars?"

Joanie shook her head. "Nope. Not at all. I like my comfy bed and pillows. Nope. No."

Jesse leaned back his head and laughed. "Darlin', you are so fun to tease. So predictable."

"I could do a trail ride if I ride in the wagon."

Jesse leaned back and looked at her. Really looked. "Miss Joanie, what is it about you and horses?"

Joanie felt her face flush. "Nothing." She looked down at her hands.

"It's something," he said softly. "It's something. Maybe you'll tell me later."

She shook her head, not trusting herself to actually say anything.

"Okay," he said in a normal voice. "How 'bout some supper?"

They walked into the dining room, where they spoke about the kinds of publicity and campaigns she was considering.

After they'd had their coffee, he suggested they look at the stars.

They started back along the walkway. The evening had cooled a little now that the sun was down. It was kind of nice to escape the heat of the day.

"Miss Joanie," Jesse said, "May I hold your hand?"

She looked at him and grinned. "You've never asked every other time you've grabbed my hand."

He laughed. His grip was warm and firm. She could feel calluses on his palm and on his fingertips. This wasn't a man who just sat behind a desk. This man worked with his body. Given what she knew now, he gave his all to his work. Probably to whatever else he was doing at the time.

She warmed all over. Especially her heart.

Jesse pointed out the common constellations and show her the app she could use on her phone that would help identify them. She took pictures, mostly to show people back home. They would never believe the clear sky here.

"Is the sky ever like this in Bawston?" Jesse asked, trying to use a Boston accent.

Joanie laughed. "That's a New Yawk accent for Baahston."

He doubled over with laughter. "Oh, that's good. Tell me more Baahston words."

She pronounced car, yard, park, all without the r's. He kept laughing.

Finally, he asked, "What keeps you there?"

"My job," she said. "Not that much else. My folks are in Florida now. It's just the job."

"Hmm, maybe you'll have to meet my family while you're out here," he said. "You sure would like them."

He walked her to her room, holding hands again.

"Miss Joanie, may I kiss you?"

She lifted her face. "I'd like that, a lot."

He bent down, grazing his lips along one cheekbone, across her nose, to the other cheekbone. "You have all those freckles, just asking to be kissed."

He gave her one last brief kiss. A real kiss—more of a promise than anything else.

"Good night, Miss Joanie."

"Don't you think you can stop with the Miss part?"

"Maybe," he said and grinned with both dimples.

She slid her hands from him, walking backward to her room. Her face aching from her forever-grin. "Goodnight, *Mr.* Jesse."

They spent the next few days like that one. She learned how to feed Queenie carrots by herself. She even started to look forward to it. Queenie had started to nicker when she saw Joanie. Joanie thought it sounded like the mare was clearing her throat; she would even nuzzle her when the carrots were gone.

At first, Joanie was uncomfortable, but Jesse convinced her to pet Queenie and she had even learned a little about grooming the mare.

Her boss canceled his visit, so Joanie had more time to do sightseeing and learn the local area. Too bad!

Jesse declared he would take her everywhere, so she could see everything.

One day, he escorted her into Santa Fe where he introduced her to the plaza where the local indigenous tribes sold their art. She bought a turquoise and sliver necklace for more than she expected to spend. But, it might be the most beautiful piece of jewelry she'd ever owned.

He introduced her to a western wear store a mile or so from the plaza, where she bought her first—and according to her—the *only* pair of boots she would ever own.

She was surprised by how comfortable they were.

He even took her to a local bar where they did do some line dancing, after a beer. She had no idea line dancing would be that much fun. But most likely it was because of her dance partner.

She was down to the last day. Jesse met her at breakfast again.

"So, time for that trail ride now?" he asked.

She shook her head. "Nope. I'll feed Queenie, but I'll take another hike instead."

He shook his head. "Joanie, I'm not sure I understand. No riding? None at all?"

"Nope," she said. "None. I'll have a great time on my hike."

His shoulders slumped. "I'm leading the ride today. I can't escort you."

She covered his hand on the table. "That's okay. I can follow a map. I'll have my phone. You have your work. Besides, you've spent a ton of time with me this past week. Do your work."

He turned his hand over and covered it with his other hand. "I'd rather spend more time with you."

"And I, with you." She shook her head. "But I need this last bit of research and you need to do your work. Meet you for dinner?"

He smiled but his dimples stayed hidden. "I'll be looking forward to it all day."

"As will I," she said, trying not to show her disappointment over his reaction.

She checked with the front desk to make sure she had the right map and started off.

This trail had ups and downs, but the first part was mostly up. Joanie encountered some people passing her going up, and some coming back down.

She felt fine and happy.

About an hour into the hike, she passed a man, sitting by himself. He had on old, torn khaki's, a dark gray tee-shirt that had seen better days, and lanky brown hair. He smelled as if he hadn't bathed in a while.

"You okay?" she asked.

He smiled and she got the willies.

"I'd be better if you were with me," he said.

"No thanks," she said and turned around. She didn't need this aggravation.

She heard him stand and follow her.

She increased her speed a little. So did he.

Well, this was not what she wanted. She was too far for help to get here fast enough. She couldn't outrun him. The trail seemed empty now. She was not going to let this idiot ruin a perfectly good hike.

"Hey, girlie," he yelled.

Oh, crap. This was unbelievable.

She was accustomed to traveling all over the world. Here, in not-quite-rural Santa Fe, she had to encounter a creep?

She increased her speed. She purposely did not turn around.

She heard his footsteps behind her. He was running. Crap.

She heard hooves in front of her. Maybe someone was riding a horse? She could hang with them for a while.

She saw Queenie cantering up to her. Queenie stopped right in front of her and did a little bow, nuzzling Joanie.

Joanie put her arm around Queenie's neck and whispered, "I'm so glad to see you. You have no idea. But I don't have any carrots."

Queenie nickered as if to say, "That's okay, you can feed me later."

"Hey, nice horse you have," the man said.

Queenie nudged her aside and stood in front of the man, ears back. Uh oh. Queenie was ready for something.

The man backed off, saying, "No problem, just having a little fun here."

Queenie advanced on him, ears back.

He walked backward up the trail.

Queenie followed him, nudging him along. He finally turned and ran.

Queenie watched him leave, and then relaxed, her ears back to their normal place.

"Now what?" Joanie asked.

Queenie neighed and tossed her head up and down.

Then, she laughed. "Oh, you want me to take you home?"

Queenie repeated the head nod.

"You know I'm afraid to ride, right?"

Queenie nodded again.

"Do you understand me?"

Queenie walked off the trail to a fallen log. She stood there.

"Wait…. You want me to use the log to get on your back?" Joanie paused. "No saddle, no bridle, no nothing?" *No way in hell, nice horse or not!*

Queenie stood there and then nodded once.

"Oh, for God's sake. I must be an idiot. I'm actually considering this."

Queenie stood a little closer to the log.

"Fine, fine," Joanie paused. "If I wasn't so scared, I wouldn't even consider this. But I really want to get back faster. And, *you* shouldn't even be here."

Queenie stomped one foot as if to say, *come on, get with the program.*

Joanie walked over to the log. She hopped up onto it and said, "Here goes nothing."

She swung her hip around, and then one leg over. She squealed, frozen half on and half off, clutching the poor mare's main for a long minute, then leaned forward to hug Queenie's neck to get on the horse all the way.

"Okay, walking only, please!"

Queenie nickered and set off for the Lodge.

Joanie sat there—or rather, jostled up and down—and thought, "I can't be doing this. I just escaped from a lunatic, and I'm riding a horse. No one would believe this.

As she approached the stables, Jesse cantered out on his horse, and slowed to meet her.

"Joanie?"

"Yes," she said, irritated and tired. She needed her water bottle.

"You're riding a horse."

"Yup."

"And, you don't have your water bottle. Want a sip from mine?"

"God yes."

Jesse extended his water bottle. Joanie took several big gulps.

They reached the stables. Jesse said, "You wait there. I'll help you off."

Joanie didn't say a word.

Jesse dismounted, and came around the front of Queenie, crooning to her, "Good girl for bringing Joanie home. We'll talk about your escape later."

"Joanie, I'm going to put my arms around your waist. You lean over and give me all your weight. I'll take you off."

Joanie slid down his body. He felt good and strong. She stayed there in the circle of his arms for a few more seconds.

"If I ever tell you I'm hiking alone again, just knock me out, okay?"

Jesse laughed, partially from relief. She was back.

"You'll have to tell me the whole story in a minute," he said. "Let's get Queenie some carrots, and you some more water."

"Okay, but I'll give Queenie her carrots," she said. "She deserves a reward for what she did."

Joanie told Jesse the entire story and then repeated it to the cops. Jesse followed her trail and retrieved her water bottle.

That night at dinner, he said, "I really don't want you to leave."

"I don't want to, either."

"Would you consider working from here while we discover what this thing is between us?"

She chewed her lip, thoughtfully. "Okay, on one condition," she said.

"What's that?"

"You teach me to ride, *really* ride."

"With pleasure. As much pleasure as this." He kissed her.

Copyright © 2019 by Johanna Rothman.

Krista writes novel length and short fiction, working in fantasy, crime and romance. She writes in a closet in Port Coquitlam, BC. Her work appears in Pulp Literature magazine, electricspec, and the Aurora-nominated 49th Parallels anthology (Bundoran Press). Her theatre background has led her to taking up audiobook narration, to being Musical Director for highschool productions (Rent, In the Heights, Anything Goes, etc.), and to co-create a play with her husband and two offspring for the Victoria Fringe Festival. She sings in two bands: FAT Jazz and the Itty Bitty Big Band.

DUCHESS KEEPS HER HEAD

by Krista Wallace

The pig, sculpted out of some smooth but velvety sort of material, stood a foot high and sat on the counter of the nurse's station. It flashed, not out of its eyes, but its entire body, at a rate of about two flashes per minute.

"What. Is. That?" the Head Nurse asked.

Duchess, fearful this might be some kind of test, said. "Looks like a pig?"

"Why's it flashing?"

"Umm," said Duchess. *What was her name again? Lorina! That was it.*

"Pack it up in a box and bring it downstairs. We can add it to the things for the jumble sale." Lorina stood in front of Duchess with her arms folded, frowning like a thunderstorm. "Things that *flash* are *not* healthy for our residents. You never know what could send an elderly person into a fit. Or a coma," she added. "Off with it!"

"Off with its head!" Duchess said with a chuckle. With her diminutive size, and general unattractiveness as a child, she had always resembled the Alice in Wonderland character whose name she shared. She had learned that book by heart, though it didn't relieve the sting from nasty comments throughout her life.

The Queen of Hearts—or rather, the Head Nurse—did not seem to appreciate the witticism. She simply glared, then was gone. Duchess shuddered.

If her superior had never seen the pig, it must be new, like Duchess. It had better not still be there when she returned to the fourth floor!

Duchess hastened to find a box in a storage closet. She lifted the pig into it, swaddling it with tissue, like a baby. She gave it a pat on the head and tried to close the lid, but then the pig flashed again, and the lid popped open.

Failure to confine the pig was not an option. This care facility was Duchess's fifth in three years, and she needed this job. If only Mrs. Jonas had been able to tell the last Head Nurse about Duchess painting her toenails for her, or if Mr. Ritesh's dementia had allowed him to let slip about the extra ice cream she had given him, maybe they'd have given her another chance. But it wouldn't do to broadcast these things. Duchess opened the desk drawer that included "tape" on the label but found none.

"Where is the packing tape?" She cursed and slammed the drawer, whipping the next one open in a frenzy. The box of paperclips, punted by inertia, flew out and splashed to the floor. A cup of coffee wouldn't have covered more linoleum.

"Dammit all to hell!" Duchess said, in what she meant to have been a mutter but turned out to be a full-on, heartfelt bellow. She pushed the chair back and it tipped over. The hips of her scrubs ripped as she knelt down and began to sweep up the little bits of curled metal with the side of her hand. She bashed her large head on the corner of the desk and yelled, "Ouch!" Reaching up to put a handful of paperclips on the desk, she knocked her coffee over.

"Oh no, oh no!" Duchess frantically grabbed Mrs. Patel's bib—Duchess had been mid-face-wipe when Lorina had called her—from the top of the desk where she had tossed it. She dabbed at the coffee in a futile effort to save the paperwork she had been filling out about Mr. Kwan's gout.

"Ahem?" a quiet male voice said.

Duchess tossed the soaked bib aside and scrunched up the now-useless paperwork.

"Yes?" she said, a little too shortly, for Duchess was only four-foot-eleven.

"Is this supposed to be in my mother's room?"

The packing tape that had eluded her was suspended above the desk by a dark hand.

"Where did you find that?" A flustered Duchess all but snatched it in her embarrassment at being caught in such an awkward position. Her gaze followed the hand up to look at the face, and she blushed an apology.

"In my mother's room," he said in a baritone voice so smooth and rich it caused vibrations in her nethers. "More or less hidden in the back of a drawer, underneath a large hardcover book, itself beneath a good many rolled up socks. Is it yours?"

She clutched the tape tightly. "Yes, it's mine… I mean, well, not mine—I was just looking for it," she bumbled. *Oh, why do I always sound like such a moron?*

Duchess's heel pressed onto a stray paperclip as she attempted to straighten up. It slid, taking her foot with it. Down to the floor she went again, but not before her broad chin smashed the desk.

The man rushed around the nurses' station and tried to grasp under her arms to help her up, looking around at the general disarray that seemed to follow her everywhere. "Oh dear, you're having quite a day."

"I don't need help—I'm fine!" she bit out through the pain. He must think she was completely useless.

He righted the chair, stepped on a paperclip and slid to the floor, clonking his head on the arm of the chair.

"For cryin' out loud." She laughed, in spite of everything. At least he looked a bit silly now, too. "I have enough to worry about. I don't need another patient."

"I'm sorry," his muffled voice came from inside his twisted jacket.

"Anyway, you're too young."

"For what?" He tugged at his jacket, his face coming back into view.

She raised an eyebrow. "To be a patient here."

"Fair enough." He crawled away from the chair and put a paperclip on the desk, then another.

Duchess finally made it to a sturdy vertical position, looked up, and up some more, at him as he rose to full height. She picked up the roll of tape.

"Who's your mother?"

"Edith Sherbrook. Obviously."

That perplexed Duchess. "Obviously? I am new at this facility as of this morning. Why should it be obvious which patient your mother is?"

It was his turn to raise an eyebrow. "Because I'm black? Because my mother is the only black woman on this floor?"

"Oh." *I should have thought of that.* "And the moral of that is—'Think before you speak,'" she said apologetically.

His eyes twinkled at her and she blushed again.

"Still, I wouldn't assume the only black resident must belong to every black person who comes through these doors," she pointed out.

He tipped back his head and laughed.

"What?" She frowned.

"I stand corrected." He inclined his head in apology, the corners of his mouth still curled up in the remnants of a smile. He moved to stand on the patient side of the nurses' station again. She could now see him without craning her neck.

"So my name is Andrew Sherbrook. My mother is Edith Sherbrook, in room 406."

Duchess was about to introduce herself, running her hands over the split sides of her trousers self-consciously, but the pig flashed, jolting the box, and panic seized her as she realized she didn't have time for socializing. Lorina could return to this floor at any minute. Duchess had been directed to package up the crazy pig thing Now Now Now, and she was determined to not lose *this* job over the laggardly following of instructions. "Okay. Is there something your mother needs?"

Andrew raised an eyebrow. "She *doesn't* need packing tape…."

"Smarty pants, are you?"

"Unless it was there for you to bind her into her bed?" He winked.

Duchess didn't reply. Her mind raced, repeating what had transpired in the last few moments. But she couldn't make sense of anything. She took a guess. "That some kind of joke, then? The moral there is—'Once bitten twice shy.'"

"No, it isn't. What's your name?"

"Meredith Duchesne. People call me Duchess."

"Why?"

"Duchesne. Duchess."

"I don't get it."

"It's a spelling thing."

"Then maybe I should see it written down."

"Did you want something?"

"Three things."

"I'm not a fairy godmother," she laughed, wishing he would hurry.

"I came here with one thing, but I keep adding to the list."

"Fine. What things?"

"To give you the packing tape."

"You've done that. Two?"

"To learn your name."

"Already done that. The last thing?"

"Will you go out for dinner with me?"

What? Why? "No."

"What have you got to lose?"

Duchess frowned. Wouldn't it be unethical to go on a date with a relative of a resident? Better not risk the Head Nurse's wrath. "I have answered three questions, and that is enough. Now be off. I must take this downstairs." She snatched the scrunched up paperwork and shoved it in around the pig in the box. "Please ask your mother why she had the tape."

The man's resonant voice continued to badger her, but in her haste and nervousness she flat-out ignored him and used her fingernail to pick at the edge of the tape so she could draw off an arm's length of it with its plasticated ripping sound. She held the box closed with an elbow and stuck one end of the tape down the side of the box, spread it over the top of the box, running it along the centre line where the flaps met, and down the far side, where she cut it off with scissors that were near to hand.

The tape she put in the bottom of the desk drawer, where it belonged.

Duchess had been mucking about at the nurse's station for far too long and the annoying yet charming fellow had long since buggered off.

She took stock of her situation. She had received an email out of the blue from Carol, the senior nurse on the fourth floor, asking her to apply for this job. It was odd to be contacted thusly, as these places followed a usual series of procedures. Clearly the Grey Havens Extended Care Community had its own system. Duchess looked it up—it hadn't appeared on any of the lists—and when she'd searched online she had to click link within link within link, down a rabbit hole of research, until she finally found a reference to it. And even that appeared in a tiny font, hidden among some illustrations. But she'd been asked to apply, and she was desperate. They asked for unusual things: a summary of her life goals, and a photo. Duchess had broken many a camera having her photo taken, but this time it had worked. The interview had gone well and she'd been hired on the spot. Now, if she wanted to keep this job she needed to keep her clumsiness under control and get cracking.

She popped the closed box on top of the counter and hurried out from behind it just as Carol emerged from Mrs. Patel's room. Carol stopped short and frowned when she saw Duchess, almost as if she had heard Duchess's thought.

"Oh, the bib!" Duchess snapped her fingers. "Lorina called me out here, and then I used the bib to mop coffee."

"That's okay, I've taken care of Mrs. Patel," Carol said with an acid tone. Her frowny, unblinking gaze went from Duchess to the box on the countertop. "What's in the box?"

Duchess looked at the box and back to Carol. "Lorina asked me to package it up."

Carol's frown deepened so far the corners of her mouth poked her jaw. She continued to not blink.

"And what is '*it*?'"

Duchess clasped her hands in front of her chest, a defensive gesture she had never managed to break. "It looked to be a decorative piece. A pig, to be precise. That flashes. Not even an umbrella stand or candy dish. Lorina said flashes are dangerous for the residents."

"Ah, yes. Except *I* like it." The pretty Filipino woman's eyes widened on the word "I" as if to emphasize it homophonically.

Duchess shrank, tempted to try to stuff her diminutive self into the box. "What's it for, then?"

"Let us just say it…will bring happiness to our residents. Now, please open the box and take it out again. Then help me bring everyone out to civilization?"

"Civilization?" Duchess, glancing behind her at the door where Lorina had exited, scurried around to fetch the scissors out of the drawer and she slit open the box.

"It's what we call the Common Area. Some of them can get here on their own, but several of our folks need our help." The clocks chimed the arrival of a new hour and, as if on cue, several bent and angular people creaked out of their doors into the corridor. "They need *your* help."

"Of course," Duchess replied. She opened the flaps of the box, pulled out the suffocated pig, and set it on the counter. It flashed twice. Duchess blinked and saw light shadows behind her eyelids. She had the strange impression that the pig was…annoyed with her.

"Sorry," she said to it.

"It's your first day. You'll love it; I promise." Carol looked pleased. Extraordinarily pleased.

"But—" She was about to ask what she should tell the Head Nurse, when a quiet whiffling sound distracted her, and she craned her neck to see if she could discover its source. Carol moved away, and so did the sound.

Duchess shrugged and followed her colleague down the bright white corridor. Involuntarily she peeked into room 406, where a male-ish pair of legs ending in boots stuck out into view. Her heart gave a peculiar flutter.

She hastened after Carol. "My schedule says today is the chair exercise session down on the third floor; will we be taking all the residents or just a few?"

Carol stopped walking and turned her head as if to look at Duchess, but didn't quite make it. Was that a hummingbird sound as her head turned? She started walking again. "Sometimes a change of routine is in order."

For clarification, Duchess said, "So we *won't* be taking them?"

Carol stopped and faced Duchess like the Queen of Hearts, and in a *Who stole the tarts?* tone, laid down the law. "Today is a day to gather in Civilization."

"I quite agree with you," said Duchess agreeably. "And the moral of—"

A woman pushing a walker stepped out in front of them. "Good morning!" she sang.

"Good morning," Duchess said, "Isn't it a fine day?"

The old woman's expression altered like someone had flipped a switch, and she snarled at Duchess. "It's a stupid day!"

"Go find a seat, Mrs. Tyler," Carol chided gently.

"Okie dokie!" Mrs. Tyler sang, and limpingly pushed her walker along, as if the grouchy interlude had never happened.

Carol looked at Duchess apologetically. "She's a piece of work, she is."

"I'll see what's for lunch!" Mrs. Tyler said, grinning.

"Good idea," Carol said.

Duchess followed Carol into Mr. McRae's room, where together they hoisted him into a wheelchair. "Let's go out to Civilization, Mr. McRae." Poor Mr. McRae almost folded over, he was so frail. "Parkinson's," Carol said, pushing a tabletop toward his chest to help him stay upright. Duchess wheeled Mr. McRae into Civilization while Carol went to gather blind Mrs. Singh from the room next door.

Duchess parked Mr. McRae against the wall, across from the elevator. She handed him a newspaper, which he pretended to read. She also slipped him a piece of chocolate, to his joy.

Mrs. Tyler rolled her walker out of the cafeteria. "Pork roast and applesauce today!" she sang. "With chocolate pudding for dessert."

"Sounds awfully yummy," Duchess said, and cringed against the upcoming mood flip from the little old woman. It didn't come. But a song did.

"Yummy yummy in my tummy!" Mrs. Tyler began, then finished with, "And then it comes…out your bummy!"

"Wow!" Duchess said with jocundity. "What a whimsical song. And the moral of that is—'Good things come to those who wait.'"

Mrs. Tyler joined the rest of the residents who had gathered in Civilization. There they all sat along the walls, poor souls: all of them old, all of them unable to care for themselves and too much for their families and loved ones to manage. *What an existence,* Duchess thought. They all stared at the pig, and Duchess wondered if Lorina had been correct that the pig was dangerous for them. Especially since the flashes seemed to be more frequent. Then Duchess noticed one person was missing.

Mrs. Sherbrook.

Duchess betook herself to room 406.

"Hey, it's the new kid." Andrew Sherbrook pulled his legs in and sat forward. "Look Mum, this is Meredith. I was telling you about her."

Mrs. Sherbrook, a jowly, wrinkled and droopy woman sat in a rocker with a crocheted afghan over her lap. Her eyes, deeply recessed in her head within bushy, protruding eyebrows and sizeable nose, peered out at Duchess as if searching for familiarity.

Duchess stepped toward her. "Mrs. Sherbrook, we're bringing everyone into Civ— the Common area. Would you—?"

"No young lady, I don't wanna go there," Mrs. Sherbrook said with a shake of her head that turned her greying black curls into aspen leaves. "Here in my room is where I am content to be. I don't hold truck with all that Community Spirit. And besides…" Here the old woman jutted her chin forward, getting as close to Duchess as she could without tipping out of the chair. "It's coming. I feel it."

Duchess, although trained to carry on conversation with the residents themselves, and not defer to their loved ones, glanced at the old woman's son. His eyes were trained on Duchess as if waiting for her response.

She looked firmly back at Andrew Sherbrook's mother. "What's coming, Mrs. Sherbrook? Lunch?"

"No, not lunch." The old woman grimaced in disgust. She turned to her son. "I thought you said this one was smart."

"I did," Andrew said.

"You did?" Duchess said. Nobody had ever called her *that* before.

"And he said you were lovely."

Duchess snapped her head around to the man's mother, and back to him. Surely these people were mocking her.

Andrew smiled in a shy sort of way that annoyed her because of the way she blushed.

"That one I'll give him," Mrs. Sherbrook said. "Birds of a feather flock together."

Duchess, who didn't understand what these people were talking about, tried to return to the point. "What is it that's coming, Mrs. Sherbrook?"

"They signed papers, you know. With a pen that *sparkled.*"

"Who? What are you talking about?" Duchess said, baffled.

"I was having none of it," Mrs. Sherbrook said. "I'm content."

"If you want to stay in here and visit with your son, that's fine with me. Did you need the tape for some reason, Mrs. Sherbrook?"

The old woman's bushy eyebrows looked like caterpillars as they rose. "I may have."

"Why don't I look into that for you?" Andrew said to Duchess.

"Fine. I have more work to do, but your lunch—"

"Is there a moral for that?" Andrew asked with a wink.

Duchess scowled. "No. Just work work work and get it done and…oh, shut up." She left the room, and leaned for a moment against wall, wondering why Andrew Sherbrook made her feel inexplicably cross. She *knew* he was just teasing her. In her experience, teasing had never been kindly meant, so it was difficult for her to convince herself that this time it was different. She pressed her hand to her heart, which was beating uncommonly quickly. Then she smiled because Andrew Sherbrook had apparently called her lovely.

Carol had shifted blind Mrs. Singh so that her wheelchair sat next to deaf Mr. Chong.

"IS IT TODAY?" Mr. Chong said to nobody in particular.

"TURN UP YOUR HEARING AID MR. CHONG," Carol said.

"NO, I CAN'T STAND ALL THE YELLING."

Only when Carol moved hunched-over Ms. Schultz away from the wall where there was lots of space and crammed her between two other people where they could pretty much use her bent back as a side table for their sippy cups did Duchess notice that the residents were all gathered quite close together. The pig's flashing was definitely more frequent. Duchess timed it. Every ten seconds.

Duchess's limbs stiffened with a fear she could not explain. She summoned every milligram of manners she could muster and turned to Carol, her hands clasped in front of her. Her hair stood on end.

Carol stood in the middle of the room, her arms outstretched. Her eyes glowed as brightly as the pig and a jet of light streamed to connect them. A sudden wind, unexpected for the inside of an extended care facility, swirled up and ruffled Duchess's hair as though she were out on the deck of a boat travelling at high speed. She had to shield her eyes from the brightness that intensified along with the wind.

"It's time!" cried all the residents, whose uplifted faces smiled with joy.

"I cannot think of a moral for this!" yelled Duchess, clutching the corner of the nursing station so she wouldn't be caught up in the wind. The pig flashed every few seconds now, faster and faster. She had a sudden feeling that the pig had something to do with this new development.

Carol began to swirl. She spun, her feet still, and she became the center of the vortex. The dazzling light burned straight through her scrubs revealing, to Duchess's great surprise, wings, like those of a giant insect. *No*, Duchess realized. *Like a fairy!*

Carol rose into the air. Where she had stood a great shaft of light touched down and splashed like silvery water falling from a great height. The residents who still had control of their large motor function stepped toward it.

"No!" Duchess cried as Mrs. Tyler rolled into the light and rose off the floor.

"Pork roast and applesauce!" Mrs. Tyler sang as she spun and became one with the beam of radiance and disappeared through the ceiling of the Grey Havens Extended Care Community.

Carol touched down again and pushed Mr. McRae's wheelchair into the light. Mr. McRae let out a *whoop* as if he were on the best roller coaster in the world.

"What are you doing?" Duchess grasped at Carol's arm, unwilling to let go of the solid piece of furniture lest she be swept away.

"I'm saving them of course!" Carol sang, as she drew Mrs. Singh into the vortex. "They all signed papers!"

"What papers?" The wind was so loud she had to yell.

One by one each and every elderly person was sucked up into the nothingness of the light.

"They all agreed to it," Carol said. "And so, my dear Meredith, did YOU!"

Horrified, Duchess tried to think through the employment papers she had signed. "I did? Why would I do that?"

"Why do you think I e-mailed YOU specifically, Meredith Duchesne?" Carol said, showing Duchess her sharp and serrated teeth. "You have no one here. You are alone. You are ugly and awkward and nobody will care when you are gone. These people…" Carol hooked her thumb upward into the light, "need you! Once they get where they are going they will be cured of all their old people ailments. They will live lengthy lives and get to enjoy the retirements of which they've been cheated by old age and illness. But until we get there, they need to be cared for. And who better than someone like you who can't hold down a job here in *this* world?"

Sadness and despair poured over Duchess.

I might as well join them.

"Yes! Come with us. We need you. And you have no family. No friends."

Duchess's insides had hollowed out like a Yorkshire pudding, and her chin sank closer to the light spilling all over the linoleum floor. Her whole life played through her mind like a movie on Fast Forward: the reactions of people meeting her for the first time, how their eyes bugged out and they literally stepped backward in horror, their struggle for words when a simple, "Hello," would not—could not—come to their lips and they settled on, "Dear God!"

Carol reached out her hand toward Duchess. A magnetic-like pull tugged her, and Duchess took a step forward.

But her hand continued to grip the edge of the Nurses' station. *Wait, wait!* she thought. *CC loves me.* Her dear fluffy cat, with its bright green eyes and large, nonjudgemental smile. Even the memory of that smile and the flick of CC's dear tail lifted heaviness from her shoulders.

"Meredith?" A gentle voice floated out of a room down the corridor.

Carol frowned, and closed her fingers into a fist, tugging Duchess another step closer. The thrum of the winds increased. Papers fluttered up and around the desk.

And Queenie, Duchess thought, remembering the other woman, who, though no beauty either, carried herself with such confidence. She wasn't always friendly to Duchess, but she had invited her to a party, which nobody else had ever done. *Good ol' Queenie.* And there had been a girl…. What was her name again? Lacie? She was sure the girl's name started with an L. She had had a nice conversation with the girl.

"Duchess, don't be a silly goose," Carol said in a sort of growl, and her eyes flashed scarlet. "There is nothing for you here. Come with us. We need you. You will be our nurse forever."

Mr. Chong, the last of the residents, shuffled into the light, his silhouette haloed by the bright pink and orange, like a sunset behind a mountain. His shriek and cackle trailed out behind him. A hearing aid dropped to the floor and bounced to stop at Duchess's feet.

Duchess took another step forward, her grip on the counter slipped. The light was so beautiful, the vortex so compelling, the thought of a new life where everyone needed her—would love her!—drew on her emotions. She longed for it and gazed up the chute into the vessel, into a New Life. She let go of the counter and stepped.

Something gripped her other hand, not roughly, but certainly with strength, with insistence.

"Meredith?" The smoothest, most velvety voice she had ever heard called her. "Duchess!"

"No!" Carol said.

Duchess turned toward the warm voice and her eyes locked with those of its owner. They were brown eyes with a hint of amber—and as warm as the pull from the portal. Duchess felt torn in half.

The hand holding hers shifted, fingers lacing between hers, weaving them closer together. "Duchess, I want to ask you a question."

"What?" Duchess had a vague memory of a conversation, quite recent, but the details refused to stop swirling about. They too were caught up in proximity of the vortex.

"Mr. Sherbrook, STOP." Carol's voice cut through the winds.

"You said I could ask three questions, and you kind of answered the last one very quickly. I don't think you gave it much thought. Duchess? Please may I ask it again, and will you think about it and answer?" His hand was strong and warm.

"Duchess, we need you," Carol intoned, her wings flapping and reflecting the gleam into Duchess's eyes. "We have a population of people who cannot manage without you. They need you to care for them. To help them get around, to dress, to bathe, to sing with them, to do exercises, so they can stay healthy until we get to my realm to cure them!"

"Duchess, I want to get to know you better," Andrew—that was it, Andrew Sherbrook—

said. "You make me smile. You bring me joy."

Duchess stared at him, and the warmth of his eyes coaxed a warmth to her belly, an unfamiliar sensation that was not unpleasant.

"You'll be a hero!" Carol sounded like a screech owl. "You'll be more than a Duchess; you could be our Queen!"

"What brings *you* joy, Duchess? What do you want? What brings a smile to your face?"

Duchess squeezed her eyes shut and shook her head. It felt good to be needed. People always like to be needed.

But on the other hand, Duchess had her own needs. Her own wants. "What was the question again?"

He laughed that golden honey laugh. "Will you please go to dinner with me?"

Duchess might have argued. She might have thought he was lying to her. After all, how could anyone want to be with her? But then she remembered CC, Queenie, the girl whose name started with L. Or was it A? They seemed to like her, awkwardnesses and all, even if it took people a while (usually) to warm up to her. She looked again at Andrew Sherbrook's eyes. Her heart swelled like a blood pressure cuff. He wasn't lying to her. A smile teased the corner of her mouth.

She was very, very tired of being *needed*. Sometimes a person needs to be *wanted*. Moreover, there were things Duchess wanted.

"The moral is—'Oh, 'tis love, 'tis love, that makes the world go round!'"

Duchess grabbed Andrew by his shirt and pulled him down toward her. She kissed him, his soft, yet determined lips sending a flash through her body. She felt electrified, awakened in places that hadn't existed before, or had atrophied. Her knees wobbling like they had been replaced by flamingoes, she immersed herself in his gaze and said, "Yes, I would love to go to dinner with you."

Andrew's face broadened with a smile which outbrighted the light from the vortex.

"NOooo!" Carol screamed as she lost control of her wings and was pulled into the eddy of lightfall. Duchess sprang forward, grabbed the pig, as bright as an arc welder, and threw it on the floor at the foot of the light. It smashed, and all its pieces were instantly inhaled. Duchess and Andrew clung to each other as the winds swirled and tried to pull them in. Instead of falling downward the light spun in an upward motion, a backward tornado. There was a loud *FWOOP!* and the light vanished, leaving behind a sound vacuum. Duchess's ears popped.

The nurse's station and the surrounding area were a mess of papers and bits and pieces, but otherwise the Common Area—Duchess didn't think she would ever refer to it as Civilization—looked as it had before, with its linoleum floor and chairs aligning the walls. Andrew helped Duchess tidy up. Simultaneously they slipped on paperclips and landed, laughing uproariously, in each other's arms.

The elevator *pinged* and the door slid open. A nurse stepped out, carrying a jacket and handbag.

"Hi, you must be Meredith," the woman said with a smile. She tucked a long strand of black hair behind her ear and reached out a hand. "I'm Seung Hee. People call me Sunny."

"People call me Duchess."

"I understand we're down to just one resident on this floor," Sunny said, and Duchess and Andrew exchanged a quick glance. He squeezed her hand and darted down the corridor to room 406. Sunny went on. "I'm sure all these spaces will be filled quickly, there is such need. And Quadrille Nursing Home is so highly recommended."

Duchess cocked her head. Quadrille had been one of the facilities she had applied to but had never heard back.

Sunny went on. "But for now I guess I'm the night shift." She grinned and plunked her belongings in the cupboard behind the station. "Have a good evening off!"

She didn't seem put out by the remaining mess. Duchess gathered her own things and joined Andrew in room 406.

His mother was sound asleep in her rocker. "I found this," he whispered. He had pulled out a drawer; taped to the bottom of it were some wadded up tissues. He had also found six buttons taped to the back of the painting on the wall. "Precious items."

Duchess smiled.

"She seems just fine," he said. Andrew adjusted the afghan on her lap.

Duchess nodded. "Content."

"Doesn't she look beautiful?" he said, drawing Duchess into the crook of his arm.

They closed her door behind them. Duchess fetched something from the nurse's station.

As the elevator descended from the fourth floor, Duchess rested her chin on Andrew's bent forearm. "I might just put my arm around your waist."

"Please do," Andrew said.

"And the moral here is—'Good things come eventually to those to whom good things otherwise had not yet happened even though the good things were waiting in and among the other things that are otherwise less good.'"

Andrew put his arm around her shoulder. "What a clear way you have of putting things," he said, teasingly.

Duchess tucked the roll of packing tape into her bag, for it was the thing that had brought them together. The elevator deposited them on the first floor, and as they passed through the front doors Duchess looked ahead with anticipation to a world of new possibilities.

An award-winning author and an Amazon bestseller under a different pen name, Olivette Devaux writes LGBT contemporary and paranormal romance. Her novel Like a Torrent, *book 2 of the Disorderly Elements Series, has won a Honorable Mention in the 2017 Rainbow Awards. She enjoys swimming the rivers in Pittsburgh, PA and can be reached at www.olivettedevaux. com.*

THOR

by Olivette Devaux

Levittown, PA was a bit of a dump (as his mom used to say), but Jayden found the world lovely now, covered in a thin layer of late March snow. Stately old maples and sycamores overshadowed the modest family ranch-style homes on their even plots, their thick trunks marching up and down the street like sentinels that marked coveted parking spots.

He made a snowball, no gloves. The white snow made his hands look dark, way past tan, and he grinned. This way, his hands were more like dad's and less like mom's, and dad was the one that stayed.

Anger washed over him. Jayden kicked against a clump his dad had left when he shoveled before he went to work. His toe stubbed a brick that froze to the driveway.

He hissed in pain and reminded himself to tell dad that his sneakers were tight again. Then he shook the pain off and took the time to soak in the pastel colors of the sunrise. Even those pallid, late winter rays lent a bit of warmth to the crisp, clean air.

A movement caught his eye.

He spun—a…wait. That couldn't have been a cat, because cats weren't that big. A raccoon? But those were never orange.

Jayden turned and ran, light-footed, on the fluffy snow until his path crossed with the footprints the feline predator had left behind.

Huge paws. Sprawling, almost tiger-like, and not sinking into the snow very much, which made him think of a nature show on animals with hair between their toes. The extra fluff held them up on the snow like snow shoes.

A roar of a bus from around the corner sent a spurt of adrenaline of a different kind through Jayden's veins. He broke for the corner bus stop, running lightly, like a cat. Like a snow cat, or a bobcat, or a Siberian tiger.

He ran like a cat that had no business prowling through a placid Philadelphia suburb.

Gustav breathed a sigh of relief when he saw a streak of orange flash across the snow in the yard. He knew Tiger would barge in through the cat door in the garage—soon he heard the click of the mechanism shutting on Tiger's tail.

He threw the basement door open. Tiger flew up the stairs, frisky and hungry and *excited*. Something had happened somewhere.

Spring, maybe.

Despite the late snow on the ground, the animals knew their seasons, and Tiger had probably found a girlfriend somewhere on the rooftops. Gustav squatted to pet his giant orange cat, taking care to scratch behind his tufted ears and to check his shoulders for signs of battle.

Tiger was a Norwegian cat, a gift from his Norwegian grandfather. The old man with his big beard and square shoulders was the last person Gustav had expected to treat him kindly when the word had spread that he was gay. "Just read the Edas," his grandfather had said, referring to the ancient Norse poems. "They talk about old warriors who gave up going a-viking and settled together in the same house. "Old cats," they called them. That's Viking retirement for you, settling down with a guy once you're done putting your mark on the world. Although…you don't have to wait till you're in your forties, like they probably had. Considering their life expectancy, an'all."

Grandpa Lund had adopted American English vernacular as easily as he adopted cats, but over the years he got selective with his cat breeds. Now he had mostly Maine Coons and Norwegians, all big and hairy and taking no lip from human or dog.

Grandpa Lund was, unfortunately, the only member of his family who had taken his coming out in stride. Scandinavia was so nonchalant about same-sex relationships, but this easy attitude didn't seem to translate to immigrants such as his parents.

His younger brother knew, but he had his own fish to fry. College was hard enough without football and the looming NFL draft complicating the issue.

But he still had grandpa Lund living off in the wilds of Massachusetts, and he had Tiger, the big orange cat. Except Tiger had taken to roaming. "Where were you, buddy?"

Tiger flipped onto his back and permitted Gustav to scratch his tummy, albeit gently. He had his way around the neighborhood, but he wasn't telling any tales.

Once Jayden came home, he tried to look for the cat footprints, but the snow had melted, and the tracks were gone. He was home alone, and as a capable eleven-year-old—almost twelve—he knew how to make himself a snack. Opening a can of tuna fish turned into gleaning a little snack for his mysterious visitor.

The trick was to hide the tuna in an old plastic yogurt container away from the driveway, where his dad wouldn't see. They were never allowed to have pets because mom was allergic to cats and dogs. But now that mom ran away with her personal trainer, and now that Jayden had been alone with his dad for three whole weeks, maybe things would look up again.

Maybe now that mom was gone, they could get a cat. A special, exotic cat with big paws and a long tail, and fabulous long whiskers. And that cat would love him, and eat food from his hand, and sleep in his bed like the cats in online videos always seem to do.

He set out the treat in the bush by the back porch, in a place where he could observe the visitor from his dining room homework spot. The frame of the antiquated French doors to the patio stuck, but there was nothing wrong with the glass and Jayden was determined to observe his visitor.

Days passed. Mom came to get her stuff, tossing her fake-blond hair and smiling too hard as she tried to convince Jayden to come live with her and Zack, the trainer. Except Jayden had met Zack, and didn't like his back-slapping, push-up pushing ways, and Mom and Zack didn't have a mystery cat. So, he stayed with dad, hoping dad would become chill and fun the way he used to be. Except Dad reminded him of a dark and sulky boat whose mooring rope had gotten loose in the fog, and who didn't know where to go, or how, or why.

More late snow fell on the spring equinox when his mom moved her last load of clothes out of the closets. Jayden was glad for its peaceful whiteness, because now he could set the tuna fish cup to the French door. It wasn't too cold out, and he forced the door open a little bit as he sat with his fuzzy slippers and a hoodie on, feeling guilty for wasting the fossil fuel heat but eager to maybe, just maybe, get a glimpse of the cat.

And maybe, just maybe, the cat would get curious and come inside.

The cat came that day. It was huge, the size of Mrs. Brenner's dog, and had wild fur tufts stick up its ears and behind its neck. Its hair was bushy and marbled with many colors, but when the sun hit it, the reds and oranges made Jayden think of the actor who played Thor in the movies.

"Thor!" Jayden whispered, keeping his voice smooth and enticing. "Wanna come in, Thor?"

Thor twitched his ears and looked around. Then he ate the tuna fish, bit by bit and with delicate precision. When he turned to walk away, Jayden noticed that Thor had a bent tail. Like it had been broken once upon a time and healed wrong, or like a thunderbolt.

Jayden smiled. In light of his lighting tail, Thor's name was even more appropriate.

Keith came home at six and brought groceries, which he and Jayden turned into dinner.

"So, what happened today?" He launched his question at his son when they were halfway through their rotisserie chicken on Italian bread and a salad.

"Not much." A standard answer. "I had to go see Mr. Hoza again, and he wanted to know about the divorce." Jayden rolled his eyes. "Why are people so nosy? I don't want to talk about you and Mom. Oh, and Taisha called. She was nosy too, but she's my older sister, so I told her about the fight you two had last time she was here."

A grimace threatened to contorted Keith's face. He drew a slow breath, fighting hard to produce a smile. Anything to wipe off that expression off Jayden's face, as though Jayden was suddenly sorry for having said that.

"It's okay, you know," Jayden said as he lightly punched his shoulder. "We do just fine, you and me. We manage like men do." He'd said it in a deep voice, one he had dropped as low as he could manage, which helped Keith crack a smile for real.

Then he listened to all the tales about school and about classes, and about that boy that asked Taisha out to a party.

But not a word about the footprints outside, or about his unusually high consumption of tuna fish.

Soon he would have to mow, Keith realized as he surveyed the backyard from his porch on this fine Sunday afternoon. The snow melted and watered the grass and spring slammed in with sun and green growth all around. The shade trees out back gave no shade yet, which suited Keith fine. Jayden could use the rays over at the park two blocks away, where he was playing basketball with a group of neighborhood kids.

What a relief.

Anything new his son did was a relief, whether it was schoolwork, or playing his guitar, or trying to coax his brown, barely-wooly hair into dreads. Even keeping an eye out for that secret cat of his was a positive activity.

Now that spring was truly here, the cat probably ran off to do its cat things and make baby cats. If Jayden was occupied with his friends and with basketball, he'd be less likely to notice when the cat decided to leave.

The divorce was now final, and Tiffany was on her way to her better partner. Zack wasn't any better than he had been, but Zack appreciated her in every single way. As an attractive woman, too, not just as a mom, or a partner, or a best friend. Keith was the first one to admit that Tiffany needed a lover who would worship the ground she walked on.

Thus, the personal trainer, Zack.

Thus, the divorce.

Keith drew a clean breath of air, relishing the scent of blooming trees even as he knew he'd pay for it with a stuffy nose later. He didn't care, for spring was here and spring was time for rebirth, for new beginnings, and for new hope.

He brushed few bits of debris from a patio chair, sat down, and turned on his phone. New beginnings meant new possibilities, he told himself as he opened a gay dating app for the first time ever.

Gustav cleaned the litter box and eyed Tiger's half-eaten bowl of dry kibble. The vet at the new office was nice, which was a good thing because he couldn't take Tiger back to Jonah, his cheatin', lyin', intern-fucking ex. Dr. Dorothy said Tiger was doing fine, though, and she even clipped his claws. "You should keep him inside," she had said. "Or at least put a collar on him with his name and your phone number, even though he's chipped."

"I know," Gustav said, well aware that such treatment would turn Tiger into a miserable, destructive tornado of feline energy. Some cats just weren't suited to the indoor lifestyle, nor to collars, and Tiger was definitely one of them.

"And if he won't let you brush his clumps out, you'll have to take him to a groomer," she continued. "His fur will get all matted otherwise."

Gustav knew that too. He also knew that taking a brush to Tiger's fur was as good as making a blood donation. Norwegian cats were closer to their wild ancestors, after all. They didn't let just anyone touch them, and Gustav would have to tease the clumps out of Tiger's coat on the sly, bit by little bit.

One thing was for sure—Tiger wasn't starving. He was either a brilliant hunter or he suckered some old lady into leaving kibble out for him.

Jayden resisted his mom's efforts to interrogate him about his dad's social life. He had just turned twelve and he was old enough to know what gay was, and why his mother had left, but that didn't mean he'd squeal on his dad and give regular reports.

She didn't need to know that his dad was out late every so often, just as he didn't need to know that his mom looked all happy and cheerful as she drank her Saturday coffee.

"So, what else is new?" She was mining for something personal. Anything would do. And Jayden knew that, because that's what Sam had said parents did after their divorce. They tried to stay close and in touch and show the kids that they were loved, which was all fine and well, but it didn't mean Jayden would tell her about dad's tighter shirts, pointy leather shoes, and the light scruff on his face.

But he wanted to give her something. "There's this cat, Mom," he said finally. "He came when there was still snow, and I think he used to sleep in the garage. He's huge!"

"He probably belongs to someone," Tiffany said.

"Not for long," Jayden said with a grin. "I'm making friends with him. You let me choose if I want to stay with Dad or with you, right? Well, I'll make his choice easier. I'll make him want to stay with me." And he proceeded to spill his plans of cat-befriending and cat-bribing to his mother.

She'd treasure his confidence and wouldn't tell his dad. She had promised, after all. Especially once she found out his name was Thor.

His cat was gone for days after the trip to the vet, which wasn't unusual in Gustav's experience. He knew Tiger would get over it and come visit his human again. He'd come for the tummy-scratches, and for the kibble, and for the way Gustav let Tiger chase the little red dot of his laser pointer.

But usual three days stretched to four, and then to five.

Gustav was feeling especially lonely, which led him to doing constructive things. Laundry was up. He opened the door to the garage to take out the garbage just when Tiger bounded up the three steps that led to the kitchen.

"Well, hey there buddy," Gustav said, and squatted to Tiger's level to greet him.

Except there was something around Tiger's neck—one of those loose plastic spring bracelets he saw in the hardware store in the cheap bin—and on it hung a tag.

It was made of cardboard and clear tape. His cat had, apparently, been adopted.

Gustav didn't know whether to be furious or amused at that little two-timing asshole. The new "owner" must've been good, though, if Tiger allowed human contact, and if he even tolerated this very light and very clever bracelet.

So much better than a collar.

Come dinnertime, Gustav served Tiger his kibble and used Tiger's distracted state to remove his makeshift collar. The tag on it was cut out of cardboard into the shape of Thor's hammer, all decorated, and it said "THOR" in capital letters. The other side of the hammer had a phone number.

A closer look at the *Mjollnir*, or Thor's hammer, told Gustav that whoever made it lacked skill, but had a lot of enthusiasm. The knotwork around Tiger's new name was drawn in determined, clumsy lines using a ball-point pen, but the name THOR was made out in a waterproof sharpie.

A kid, probably.

Gustav thought back to Tiger's heritage and smiled. Thor was a fairly good name for Tiger, but it was one Gustav would've never considered using himself. He didn't, after all, see his church-going neighbors name their cats and dogs "Jesus."

He reached for his own necklace and felt the sterling silver Thor's Hammer warm against his skin. The hammer connection, and the fact that Tiger made new friends, took some of the sting of Gustav's newly single state. Perhaps he should go meet this family. If Tiger liked them, then they were made of sterner stuff, or perhaps of exceeding patience.

Moreover, nobody was going to steal Gustav's cat.

Keith was spreading mulch around the pansies he and Jayden had planted by the front walkway. The brilliant green of the fresh-cut grass gleamed like a jewel in the afternoon light, and Jayden's excited voice filled Keith with more hope for the future than his dating app attempts had to date.

It was okay to be single, after all. Just because he wasn't feeling the chemistry he and Tiffany needed to make their marriage work, he didn't need to dive into the gay dating pool. Or any dating pool at all. "It's just you and me, buddy, and we're a team," he said to Jayden, who looked up at him.

"Gimme five, Dad!"

Their dirty hands slapped until mulch bits flew, making Jayden laugh. And making Jayden laugh was the best reward of all.

"That looks really good," a strange voice said behind them.

They both turned as one. Keith stood and brushed his hands off his jeans. Suddenly he felt conscious of the grime under his fingernails and of his loose, torn, and filthy jeans he reserved only for yard work. His superhero T-shirt, the one with a black panther on

it and the words "Wakanda Lives," had been a gift from Jayden so, naturally, he had to wear it on their day together.

Now he was conscious of soiling a gift, as well as looking like a sweaty hot mess in front of a drop-dead gorgeous stranger.

"Hi, I'm Gustav and I'm here about the cat."

Jayden stiffened next to Keith. "About my cat Thor?" His voice was apprehensive, and Keith drew himself to a greater height. Nobody would make his son come to hurt over that cat.

Gustav smiled at Jayden and pulled a slinky bracelet out of his pocket. Hanging off it was that quirky Thor's hammer name tag which Jayden had made only a few days ago.

Keith bristled.

"It seems that your cat Thor is my cat Tiger," Gustav said. "And it also seems that he likes visiting between our houses. I'd like to talk with you," he nodded at Jayden, acknowledging him, "and with your…dad?" He cocked his head with a question in his eyes, to which Keith nodded an affirmative. "I want my cat, and you want my cat. Your cat wants both of us. What we need to reach is some kind of a compromise."

Jayden thought he would break into tears when the stranger pulled Thor's bracelet out of his pocket, but when Gustav had made eye contact, he sucked in a breath and straightened up just like his dad.

He wouldn't cry. Tears never got him what he wanted.

And then Gustav talked about his cat, and *his* cat—it sounded awfully familiar.

"So you want joint custody, like Dad and Mom have of me?" he asked, seeking some kind of a familiar framework.

His dad nudged him. "Slow down, son," he said, but his voice was curiously pinched. "I'm Keith."

"And I'm Jayden," Jayden piped up.

"And I'm also kind of dirty, but we just finished up. If you let me clean up a bit, maybe we could sit on the patio and talk. That's where Thor likes to hang out."

Gustav's face brightened, which made his red-blond hair look like the halo of the sun. "Thanks, that would be awesome. I don't want to inconvenience you—just take your time."

Keith led Gustav around the house and to a concrete patio covered with a roof. The sliding glass door was fixed now—one of those projects on an endless to-do list—and he nodded to it. "We go in this way, but we take our shoes off. There's no mud room, so the boot tray is a bit of a compromise. You want anything to drink? Beer? Water?"

"I'll have whatever you're having, thanks," Gustav said as he glanced at the glass table with four padded chairs. "Take your time, I'll just hang out here and see if Tiger shows up."

"If Thor shows up," Jayden piped up from where he was kicking off his muddy sneakers.

Keith didn't comment. He raced up the stairs, ripping his clothes off like they were on fire. That man was *fine*, he had the build and the smile and everything.

And he had acknowledged Jayden's presence as well as his interest in the cat, which was, of course, the most important thing.

Keith jumped in the shower for a quick cold rinse, just to get the dirt and mulch from behind his ears, where it inevitably landed after a few hours of playing in it. Once he dried off, he yanked his drawers open and peered at the best prospect.

Clean everything, even underwear. Not that the new guy would ever know, but this was about Keith's confidence, and he didn't mind a little boost.

His skinny jeans. The black ones that showed off his ass.

A button-down shirt with a pale lavender stripe and a coordinating paisley design on the inside of the cuffs, the collar, and the placket. A glance in the mirror gave Keith a satisfactory first impression of a hopefully hot dark-skinned gay man with a head of close-cropped wooly hair and his sleeves rolled just high enough to showcase his muscled arms.

Maybe he should get an earring.

Someday.

He slipped into a pair of leather loafers, the ubiquitous "boat shoes" so popular in the area and skipped back downstairs. On the way to the kitchen he stuffed his phone in his pocket and grabbed two bottles of the latest IPA microbrew and a root beer.

"Wow, Dad," Jayden whispered behind him. "Why you all dressed up?"

" 'Cause we have a guest," Keith said with a calm he didn't feel. "Come on, go get a glass with ice if you want any."

Even though Gustav came here just to talk about Tiger, he couldn't shake the feeling that the divorced dad—thank you, Jayden—might be batting for his team. He really wanted Tiger, but Jayden was obviously distressed at the thought of losing him, and after all…that cat was his own person in so many ways.

Gustav couldn't avoid sharing him unless he locked Tiger inside, which would turn the poor animal into a miserable, neurotic wreck.

His best bet was a friendly compromise.

Except Jayden had a hot, divorced dad, who looked super adorable with dirt smudged on his high cheekbones and with bits of mulch on his shoulders and in his hair. This would complicate the negotiations as much as Jayden being a cute kid with enough patience to befriend a cat who was still, genetically speaking, half wild.

Gustav's thoughts drifted back to Keith. He was willing to bet that he had carried the bags of mulch on his formidable shoulders and that one of the bags got ripped—and how did a bit of gardening dirt become, all of a sudden, so sexy?

He settled on the tube-and-mesh patio chair's waterproof cushion and leaned back to observe. A blanket of Sunday peace had descended over the neighborhood, the kind where even the grass dudes hesitated to fire up their lawnmowers. This was quite different from his duplex apartment halfway between here and Main Street. The yards were bigger, the street was wider, and the dark rhododendron bushes with their swollen buds provided a lovely evergreen foundation planting.

"Thanks for waiting," he heard Keith said as he nudged the sliding door open with his hip. "No, no, don't get up, I got it."

Gustav got up anyway and closed the door after Keith. He eyed the bottles in his hand. "Beer, huh?"

"Not a fan?" There was no judgment in Keith's voice.

"I'm a fan, but I don't know this brand." Gustav opened the door again to let Jayden pass.

"No sign of Thor?" Jayden asked, looking around.

"Not yet."

"No problem," Jayden said. "Sit still. He doesn't like sudden movements. I'll be right back."

"Quite a kid you got there," Gustav said with a smile once Jayden disappeared into the house. "And quite a cat whisperer." Now that he looked Keith over again, trying not to be obvious, he relished the vision of an entirely different person. The sexy gardener with endearing dirt smudges was replaced by an assured man of the house—and was he wearing *lavender*? Assured for certain. "Great shirt, by the way," he said, no longer bothering to hide his appreciation. "I don't think I could pull that off."

Keith squinted at him, both as though to see whether he was being made fun of, but also with an assessing look. "Green," he finally said. "Green or aqua. Lavender would be a stretch for you."

And dammit if Gustav didn't feel heat rush to his face.

Jayden rescued him from further embarrassment when he appeared with a yogurt cup in his hand. "If he's around, he'll come for this," he said with a smug grin.

"Yogurt?" Gustav didn't hide his alarm. "You know he gets diarrhea from dairy, right?"

"No, tuna!" Keith said with a chuckle. "We don't have a litter box set up for him. That seems to be your job!"

And that's how their negotiations began. Tuna fish was okay, but only as an occasional treat. Kibble was healthy for his teeth and gums, dairy was a no-no. "He likes this one brand of cat treats," Gustav volunteered, knowing he was giving the competition an unfair advantage.

Then a shadow moved, and the three of them stilled as a giant orange cat surveyed the scene.

He paused at seeing them together. Then, slowly, paw by paw as though he was hunting in the shelter of the foundation plantings, he approached his tuna fish treat.

Hungrily, he ate.

"Act natural, guys," Jayden prodded them. "He should get used us moving and talking. Just not too fast and not too loud."

"That's right." Gustav gave Jayden an approving smile, then met Keith's veiled gaze. He lifted his beer. "To the joint custody of Tiger."

"To the joint custody of Thor," Jayden said with a mischievous smile.

Once they toasted and drank, Gustav pulled out his own Thor's hammer necklace and let it flash in the shady daylight of the patio. "Not everyone thinks Thor can be kept as a pet," he said with a soft murmur.

The sight of the Thor's hammer on the cat had been fine. Probably just a by-product of watching too many movies and reading the comics. Keith bristled when he saw it on Gustav's necklace, though.

He'd read about people like that. People who worshipped the old Norse Gods and thought of themselves better for it.

Purer. *Whiter.*

And that would never do—except, since Gustav had obviously hit the right note with Jayden and since there was this unexplainable charge between Gustav and himself, he took a mental step back and assessed the situation. He'd give his guest the fullest benefit of doubt.

"What does the hammer mean to you personally, Gustav?"

He saw Gustav flinch. "Oh, Gods. I can tell you exactly what you're thinking of right now."

Something tight loosened within Keith's chest. "Go ahead, try me." His voice was soft and melodious, like he was coaxing Gustav from under the bed. As though Gustav himself had turned into a shy cat who didn't want to get his fur brushed out.

"I came by it honest," Gustav started out. "My parents moved here from Norway and I was born here, but my grandpa has always told me stories of the ancient Gods, and, well. They make as little sense as any other deities, and if I'm going to think of a Higher Power, at least this is personal." He paused. "They are familiar to me, like friends from when I was a kid."

"So it's not…." Keith trailed off, hesitating. Not wanting to accuse.

"I'm definitely not a member of some crazy white supremacist group, no. I know they exist." A stubborn expression took over Gustav's face. "They would have no use for someone like me. They don't know the first thing about real Norse history, and they think gay men don't belong in that world."

"You're gay?" Jayden, of course, had to act his age just at the wrong moment.

"Jayden." Keith tried to reign him in. He didn't want Gustav to feel unwelcome or judged. Keith had skirted too close to doing just that himself.

Gustav forced a little laugh. "No, it's okay. Really. Yes, I'm gay and out." He shrugged like it didn't matter, like he didn't bare his soul to yet another pair of strangers.

Keith was all too aware what that was like. At least Gustav didn't say "How'bout you," because Jayden didn't know yet. Hell, Keith was still wrestling with the whole issue. His left ring finger was still thinner than the others from the wedding ring he used to wear for thirteen years, and old habits die hard.

"Well…I better get going." Gustav finished his beer and got up.

"Stay for dinner," Keith blurted out. "I'm making burgers, nothing special, but it would be great to have company!" He glanced at Jayden, who brightened.

"Yeah, have dinner with us! We have ice cream for later. And we can feed Thor here." He said the last with a sly, calculating look.

"Please," Keith added, and leaned back. Now it was up to Gustav to make up his mind.

So the divorced dad wasn't out to his son. Interesting. They both wanted him to stay, though. Keith had even said "please," like serving him hamburgers was some kind of an honor.

He felt welcome, and not just because of his cat.

"It would be my pleasure." He sat back down. "On one condition. You'll let me help."

"Sure," Jayden agreed readily in that *what you see is what you get* way of eleven-year-old boys.

Keith's smile warmed his face all the way to his eyes. Gustav was getting drawn into his gaze, relaxed and excited both at once. Tiny lightnings sparked in his veins just by being here, being close to Keith and also to Jayden, and to their shared-custody cat who sunned himself on a dark, warm patch of dry mulch not far away.

"Dad?" Jayden's voice bore a cautious note.

"Um." Keith broke off and floated back down to Earth, focusing instead on the little man who sat there, all restrained and waiting. He hesitated, well aware this was probably not the best time to have *the* conversation, but inspired all the same by the distracting presence of Gustav. He needed his son to hear it from him first, rather than get confused by the chemistry clearly sparking between him and the Norseman. "I have something to share, son."

Jayden gulped. Apprehension widened his eyes.

"Jayden, when your mother and I divorced, it meant that we can also date other people. Like she's dating Zack."

Jayden nodded. "Okay?"

"What I didn't share with you is that I sometimes like to date men."

Jayden tilted his head, considering what he had said. "Like Gustav? 'Cause Dad, you two keep acting like you want to ask each other to the school dance." He shuddered dramatically. "You're as gross as Mom and Zack! But…if you to get together and be all gross, I get to keep Thor fulltime!"

Emotions chased across Keith's face. Terror and embarrassment, stubborn pride and relief. Gustav had a sudden urge to get up, walk over, and hug him from behind.

Keith had come out to his son. He'd said the words, and he got a reaction, and the world was still spinning on its axis.

"Now, Gustav might not want to 'get together' with me," Keith felt dutybound to point out, "but at least…well…."

"If your dad and I become boyfriends, we'll be a lot more gross than your mom and Zack," Gustav said slowly. "I don't know, is Tiger worth that to you?"

"Not Tiger, *Thor*," Jayden said. "Tigers look different anyway. They're a different species." Then, quietly, "He's worth it."

He didn't say who.

"Suppose you combine the names somehow," Keith suggested into the awkward silence. "Not Tiger or Thor, but Tighor? Or Thorger? And he'd still recognize it. It would have to sound similar enough, so he isn't too confused."

"He won't be confused," Gustav and Jayden said at the same time, then burst out laughing.

"How about it, Jayden?" Gustav leaned forward, all serious. "Can we compromise on a name we can both live with?"

"Tighor," Jayden said. "That sounds closer to Thor."

A thunder rumbled from afar. As they all stood up and walked to the edge of the patio to inspect the sky, a dark cloud loomed beyond the still-leafless trees. One of those spring storms that were dime a dozen in the area, rolling off the Atlantic. The timing couldn't be beat, though.

"Even Thor approves," Keith said.

Gustav smiled and fingered the silver pendant under the fabric of his T-shirt as fat, warm droplets began to splatter on the fresh mulch and growing grass, drumming on the patio's roof. "He does," he said. "But Tighor doesn't. Look at him scamper to where we are!"

Saturday was a gym day, and the gym was air-conditioned. A good thing, too. The humidity outside was summer-camp quality even though the school year had just ended. As Jayden joined his mom and Zack in a set of push-ups and sit-ups, his mom kept asking her subtle, probing questions between sets.

Is everything okay?

Are you lonely?

Are you two eating right?

Zack seemed entirely focused on his form, paying them no heed whatsoever. Or giving them privacy.

"It's good, Mom. We're fine." Then, because it had been a few weeks and his dad had suggested to Gustav that he might as well follow his cat and move in, he said, "Dad and Gustav are making broiled fish since I don't like it and I'm with you and Zack this weekend. And since Tighor's gonna eat the leftovers anyway."

"Going to, not *gonna*," his mother corrected him automatically, the way she always used to do before the divorce. Hearing her do it again was surprisingly reassuring. "So, tell me about this Gustav."

Zack looked up from the half-sit-up position he had been holding, winked at Jayden, and smiled.

A cold, fearful chunk Jayden didn't even realize he carried in his chest melted into a sense of profound relief. He wanted to tell them how Gustav played his guitar, how he taught him to solve for x, how he and his dad cooked together. How neither of them

let him watch "Kill Bill" yet, and how his dad started playing basketball with Jayden again.

He cranked out a few more push-up, sat up, and said with all the dignity he could muster: "He's okay."

Copyright © 2019 by Olivette Devaux.

Amanda Pillar is an USA Today *bestselling author and award-winning editor who lives in Victoria, Australia, with her husband and two cats, Saxon and Lilith. Amanda has had numerous short stories published and has co-edited the fiction anthologies* Voices *(2008),* Grants Pass *(2009),* The Phantom Queen Awakes *(2010),* Scenes from the Second Storey *(2010),* Ishtar *(2011) and* Damnation and Dames *(2012). Her first solo anthology,* Bloodstones, *was published by Ticonderoga Publications in 2012. The award-winning sequel,* Bloodlines, *was published in October 2015. Amanda's first novel,* Graced, *was published by Momentum in 2015. The stories* Captive *and* Survivor *were also released in 2016, followed by* Bitten *and* Ashes *in 2017. She has just started the exciting new Heaven's Heart series, with* Deadly Passion *and* Benevolent Passion *published in 2018. In her day job, she works as an archaeologist. Readers can sign up to Amanda's mailing list for future news and free reads by visiting www.amandapillar.com for regular writing updates.*

STOLEN SECRETS

A Heaven's Heart Story

by Amanda Pillar

CHAPTER ONE

A thousand years ago

Fear was for the weak.

And Baal was not weak.

Stupid, however, he may have been stupid.

His current accommodations were tiny—a mere ten feet by ten feet. But it was filled with a range of instruments all designed to elicit terror: chains, whips, knives, an instep borer, and his personal favorite, the scavenger's daughter—the counterpart to the rack. Too bad for his captors that Baal was familiar with each and every device, having used many of them himself.

You could not fear what you already knew.

Although, he did not particularly wish to experience them firsthand himself. Pain was, after all, pain: he did not relish the experience. Carefully, he tested the strength of the chains that were looped around his wrists and feet, then cursed mentally. They had been magically reinforced. His captors had been prepared for his kidnapping, it was clear.

After all, a god was no easy thing to abduct.

The door to his cell slammed shut and footsteps approached. "Your Hell-lord cannot save you." The gloating voice belonged to Satan, ruler of Inferno.

Baal didn't bother wasting precious oxygen on the reply.

The part-god, part-human male strode into Baal's line of sight—red light flickered over his embroidered silk tunic, which hung below his knees. His long hair was tied back, and his endlessly dark eyes sparkled with amusement.

This was nothing more than a game to the Hell-lord.

And the reason for the game?

The woman standing at Satan's left elbow.

Her long black hair shone with health, while her almond-shaped eyes had a flat, deadened appearance. She tilted her chin upward when she noticed Baal's regard. Iyo, former Queen of Wa, was Satan's half-sister and his current favorite toy.

And now Baal had been forced to join their fun.

Although, he wasn't sure how much enjoyment Iyo received from playing torturer. Rumor had it that Satan was courting his sibling, and that she had been enslaved into his service. He couldn't see a slave-brand on her, but then, only her arms and neck were exposed.

"What?" the Hell-lord taunted. "You think that Lucifer will come and save you?"

"No," Baal finally replied. "You know he can't. The law forbids it."

Baal was one of Lucifer's Great Dukes. In Sheol, Lucifer's realm, he was untouchable by Satan or Hades, the ruler of Tartarus. But here, in Inferno? Satan's will applied. The fact that Baal had been kidnapped from the Human Realm while on business for his lord, that was incidental. He had been foolish enough to get taken.

Satan's gleeful expression darkened, and he jerked a hand at his half-sister. "Torture him for answers."

The former queen stepped forward, her hand hovering over a table covered in various sharp objects. "Answers to what questions?"

"The usual." Satan then stepped to the only door in the room.

She nodded and picked up a blade.

"Oh," Satan turned back to them. "I want his face cut up. I don't like it."

The Hell-lord left.

Baal settled back against the wall. The rock pressed into his back, almost comforting. So, Satan didn't like the look of his face?

Iyo spoke, her voice flat, "He gets jealous easily. He doesn't like me spending time with handsome males."

Baal met her gaze. A brief spark of anger flared to life on her face, before it returned to its prior emotionless.

Reaching out with his thoughts—a gift from his Murmur demon father—he tried to find a way into her mind. But it was closed away, hidden behind impenetrable shields. He would not be able to influence her.

"I'd apologize for this, but it would be a waste of breath," she said, moving closer, the light catching on the blade. "Because I'll do it again, if I have to."

Baal nodded. Her explanation was more than he had expected.

She bent down, tilting his chin up, running the flat of the blade against his cheek. "Tell me Lucifer's secrets."

"No."

She smiled then, the expression filled with melancholy.

"Let us begin."

This is going to hurt.

CHAPTER TWO

Present day

Laird, formerly the god Baal and a Great Duke of Sheol, didn't believe in favors. There were three reasons for this:

One: favors didn't earn coin;

Two: people often forget they owed you anything; and

Three: he didn't want to earn a reputation for helping people.

Every now and then, however, he found himself on the verge of doing someone a favor. Normally, he talked himself out of such nonsense, but one day, ten years ago, he had gone against his instincts and helped a tired and scared female 'cambion.'

Today, it appeared she was paying him back.

His assistant stuck her head around the door to his office, her large, limpid eyes apologetic. "Mr. Daemon, I'm sorry, she just appeared—"

Asha Himm, second-in-command to Hades, the Hell-lord of Tartarus, crossed her arms over her chest. She stood just inside the doorway, her black boots stark against the pale wooden floors. "I made an appointment."

The Tortas demon glanced down at her tablet and blinked rapidly. "I swear, it wasn't there a minute ago—"

Laird waved a hand from his desk. "It's fine, Goldie. You may go."

The demon shut the glass door behind her, the tortoiseshell pattern on her skin standing out in stark relief against her white shirt. He could feel her confusion and irritation as she returned to her desk.

Asha moved forward and took a seat, crossing her legs at the knee. Her long hair glinted blue-black in his office lighting, and her hazel gaze was direct. She'd grown in power and confidence since he'd last seen her. "I hope your assistant isn't too angry."

"She will get over it." That was the beauty of Tortas demons: they may not be the most vicious, but they prized efficiently over almost everything else. Goldie would spend the next hour prioritizing the rest of the day for him, to account for the unexpected appointment.

A smile quirked the corners of Asha's mouth, before her expression turned serious. "I came here to deliver a warning."

"I thought as much."

Her eyes flared in surprise. "Oh?"

"Rumor has it that someone may have put a hit out on me." Laird was used to such antics. As the CEO of Three Circles Recruitment Agency—one of the only seven such agencies in all the realms—he was responsible for placing demons in a variety of different job positions. Some demons didn't like being sent back to Hell, and some didn't like the positions they were given.

He had survived at least a hundred previous attempts.

He would survive a hundred more.

"You have good intel," she acknowledged, then she flicked her fingers, and black fire laced the corners of the office. An anti-eavesdropping spell. She *had* grown more powerful in the last decade. "But did you know that Satan is the one who issued the hit?"

Laird's expression didn't change, but shock made his blood pound in his head.

Not possible.

"No, that I had not heard," he said slowly.

His appointment as CEO of the recruitment agency had meant he was supposedly untouchable by the three rulers of Hell. Skies, he had given up his *godhood* to take the position and the safety it secured.

"Do you know why?" Laird asked.

Asha sat back in her chair. "Do you remember who I am, yet?"

He glanced at her sharply. "I've always known who you were."

"You said you didn't remember, the last time we spoke." A decade ago, in this very office. She had been searching for a job, he had wanted to refuse to help her. The scars on his face, had, after all, been her doing. His office had been renovated since then, but he hadn't changed. Was unlikely to at this stage in his long life.

"Well," he allowed, "the woman I met here was scared and lonely. She bore little resemblance to the one who had tortured me in Satan's cells."

Asha swallowed. "I am sorry about that. But the scars—they suit you."

He ran a finger over his cheek. They had been there for the past thousand years, and yet, he was somehow still occasionally surprised by them when he looked in the mirror. "So, what does your identity have to do with Satan's hit?"

"He worked out you were the one to arrange my interview with Hades."

Laird frowned. "It took him *ten years* to discover that?"

The Hell-lord's spies needed to be sacked.

"It took him ten years to work his way around the contract that means he can't harm someone in your position."

That made more sense.

Hell-lords might be evil, but they abided by the rules like zealots did a religious text. "Do you know what loophole he discovered?"

"If one of his lackeys hires the hit at their own personal cost and discretion—without being ordered to, or without prompting—then Satan is not responsible."

"These contracts need to be amended." He'd speak to a lawyer ASAP. However, in the meantime, it meant a hired killer would be on Laird's trail. An angry demon was one thing, an organized hit with money behind it, another.

"I agree. But you need to get extra help."

"Extra help? With what?"

"Security."

He laughed. "I am a former Great Duke of Sheol and a Murmur demon. I will be fine."

"Rumor has it that Satan's lackey has hired the Lamia Guild, the Xargi and the Merry Men."

All assassination guilds with fierce reputations. The Merry Men's was the worst. They liked to preserve the bodies of their victims.

"They are all Inferno guilds."

"Lucifer forbid any of his assassins to take the job, as did Hades."

At least he knew his former master still remembered him fondly.

Her gaze grew direct. "Hades has also recommended a particular guild for bodyguard detail."

He tried not to be insulted that the former god did not believe in Laird's ability to take care of himself. "Yes?"

"The Halcyon Guild. They are renowned for their abilities—paired with the Fallen Star mercenary group, one of their assassins recently beheaded Set."

Set, the ancient Egyptian god who lived in Inferno. They'd once been contemporaries: Laird a storm god, Set a chaos deity. They had not, however, been friends.

"According to you," Laird said, "I don't need an assassin, I need a bodyguard."

"They provide those, too." Asha stood and glanced down at her watch. "I have to go, but look them up. The assassins will be on you soon enough."

He nodded. "Thank you."

She met his stare, her face solemn. Absently, she raised a hand to her cheek—the same side that bore the scars on his own face. "It is the least I could do."

She teleported out of his office.

His intercom rang. "Mr. Daemon, your next appointment is here."

"Tell them I will be ready in five minutes," he replied, no doubt frustrating his assistant all over again. Focusing on his computer, he quickly searched for information on the Halcyon Guild.

There.

For enquiries, call Trick on HALCYON 666.

CHAPTER THREE

Sylvester didn't have many friends. So, the fact his demon master, Trick, had just sold one of them, well, it was suffice to say that Sylvester was pretty annoyed.

To say the least.

"She won't last in the Mortus den, you know that," he growled at his boss.

Trick, golden-haired bastard that he was, just shook his head. They were standing in the entry foyer to the Halcyon Guild building, the large stone walls soaring high above them, the scent of ozone and sulfur strong in the air.

A group of Mortus demons had just summoned a Devilsgate and left, his buddy Peony with them.

"Dru wasn't here," Trick said, "and I wasn't about to sell her to them."

"Because you want to fuck Dru, whereas Peony doesn't tickle your fancy."

Trick glared. "Watch it."

Peony was the guild's medic and Sylvester's boss when he was on nurse duty. Dru—Peony's identical twin sister—was one of the scariest people he'd ever met. Sylvester got along with Dru, but Peony was his friend. He'd tried to help her as best he could when he could, but he lived and worked in a den of assassins. Kindness could get you dead.

Trick spun on his heel. "Come with me."

Grumbling under his breath, Sylvester followed. He didn't have to like his boss to work with him, but it would have been a nice bonus.

They came to a stop at Trick's office—a room that was barely used. Trick did most of his business in the great hall, that way everyone knew when he was happy and when he was not. Things tended to end badly when their boss was angry.

Entering the room, Sylvester took in the single desk and chair and crossed his arms over his chest. "What do you want?"

"So polite."

"You don't pay me for my manners."

"True." Trick sat in the sole chair. "I have a job for you."

"One that requires us to use your office?"

"Yes. I was made aware by Hades himself that this was to be kept quiet." He paused, as if thinking about his next words. "I have been approached by one of the recruitment agencies' CEOs."

Surprise zinged along Sylvester's nerves. The recruitment agencies were almost untouchable—their roles vital to the three circles of Hell. Why did one of their CEOs need to hire a thief or an assassin?

"And what do they want?" he asked.

Trick tapped a long finger against the desk. "Protection. Bodyguard duty."

Sylvester let his arms fall to his sides. "So why have they contacted *us*?"

"It *is* one of the services we offer, although not one of the more common ones."

The Halcyon Guild was renowned for cleaning up other people's messes and stealing a little bit of gold on the side. But, for a price, you could have almost any other service you wanted—even escort duties. Trick believed in diversification.

"Why tell me?" he asked. While Sylvester did do the occasional assassination, his expertise was in breaking and entering—or visiting and pilfering, as he liked to call it.

"Because I think you are best suited to the job, due to your…genetics."

"Which part of my genetics?" he asked as tingles spread along his spine. Not many people knew the truth about Sylvester's origins, but Trick did. Sylvester was a human/demon hybrid; however, he wasn't just any old cambion: his father had been a hybrid, too. Sylvester was the rarest of the rare: a cambion born to a cambion. And his father was half-Murmur demon, while his mother was pure Pollus.

"The Murmur."

Everyone in the guild knew about his Pollus ancestry, since he had a natural healing ability, but no one knew about his half-Murmur father. Mind readers and manipulators weren't exactly…popular amongst the demon set. Although, he'd never been able to read Trick's mind: it was hidden behind a wall of gray mist.

There was only one Murmur demon living in the Human Realm that Sylvester knew about—the head of Three Circles Recruitment Agency. He'd never met the man, since he didn't make a habit of interacting with other Murmur demons; they'd sense what he was and kill him for it.

Murmurs didn't like cambions. At all.

"You do realize he will kill me if he learns what I am?"

"One, there will be a stipulation in the contract that he cannot attack you, now or in the future. And two, well, Mr. Daemon isn't your regular Murmur demon."

"Clearly not, if he needs a babysitter." Their minds were so powerful they could strike killing blows with their telepathy. They didn't need to touch an enemy to end them.

Trick's brown eyes flashed. "There have been three guilds hired to assassinate him. That would make anyone jumpy."

He let out a low whistle. "Who'd he irritate to warrant that?"

"Satan."

Sylvester winced. *I need a drink.*

The Casa de los Condenados was a bar located just within the border of Sheol, the Hell realm ruled by Lucifer. It was so close to the Human Realm you could almost smell the pollution, rather than the sulfuric scent of the underworld. The wood and stone building looked more like an old manor house than a pub, but inside, there was a long bar that stretched almost the entire length of the ground floor room, and a series of tables organized before it.

The room was packed, as always; it was why this place was Sylvester's chosen hangout. Alcohol, drugs, sex, and information were all sold here, with the latter at a premium. And it was information that he

valued the most. He'd read the dossier on Mr. Daemon, although it hadn't been particularly detailed. It had listed the male's species, occupation, and current risk status. Sylvester was more interested in the parts the file had skipped, like age, power, and history.

Why did Satan want the demon killed?

And how had the Hell-lord managed to get around the contract that stated recruitment agency owners or managers were exempt from Hell's politics?

Of all the Hell-lords, Satan was perhaps the most underhanded. Rumor had it that Lucifer was cunning, while Hades was about as complex as a brick to the face. Sylvester liked the style of Tartarus' Hell-lord the most—at least with a brick, you had a chance of dodging.

Striding through the crowd, Sylvester rapped his knuckles against the polished wooden bar. The female bartender flicked him a glance and continued to serve the winged Infernus demon who'd been placing his order. Sylvester eyed the horned demon and fought a grimace. He didn't like their kind much—evil to the bone, they'd sell their own mother if it could make them a profit. And while Sylvester was a thief, there was one thing he understood above all else: loyalty. It's why he hadn't walked out on Trick the moment the guild master had sold Peony. He owed Trick, and he wouldn't forget it.

"Can I have a martini, but with an extra olive?" Someone asked next to him, the voice like rolling thunder.

Sylvester turned slightly toward the speaker and did a double take. The man was hot. *Beyond* hot. With dark red hair swept back from a widow's peak and steely brown eyes, the guy looked like a GQ model, except for the delicately curving horns that crowned his head. The demon pivoted, exposing the other side of his sharp profile. Crisscrossing scars decorated one cheek, almost as if the other man had been branded.

If anything, the scars made him more beautiful.

"Like what you see?" the demon asked, noticing Sylvester's stare. A flicker of heat flared in the other demon's eyes.

"I do."

A low chuckle emerged from the stranger, making the blood pound in Sylvester's head and butterflies erupt in his belly. There was something magnetic about this demon; something that compelled Sylvester to learn more, *want* more.

"What are you after?" The bartender's request cut through the moment, and Sylvester turned to the Foraci demon, annoyed that the short interlude with the stranger was over. Instant connections like that were few and far between in his life.

Another time.

That was if the other demon ever came back to the bar while Sylvester was there.

You're here for information, not sex. You aren't meant to be having one night stands anymore, anyway.

Since his mother's species, the Pollus, were part-Incubus, it made picking up too easy. He'd decided it wasn't all that fun to make a conquest, rather than a date, and, well, he wasn't really a dating kind of guy.

He realized the bartender was staring at him impatiently, her slit-pupiled eyes narrowing as the seconds ticked by. Other demons hollered for attention.

"Can I get a glass of wine?" he asked quickly.

"White, red or bloody?"

"White."

"House okay?"

"Sure."

She handed him a glass of shimmering pale liquid—clearly a distant relative of human-made wine—and he paid and turned, figuring that the sexy demon had disappeared to find a table. But no, the male was a few steps away, sipping slowly at his martini. Sylvester took a large mouthful of wine while he briefly argued with himself. The taste of grapes and mulberry was instant, along with the fiery tingles of a spell.

What have they drugged this with?

A feeling of contentment began to seep through his limbs.

Anti-fighting spell.

He should have figured.

With this many demons in the room—complete with Infernus guests—the bar was probably taking no chances.

Looking up, Sylvester made eye contact with the scarred demon.

Talking to the guy isn't sleeping with the guy.

No. He could do the meet and greet, maybe even get his cell number….

No. Try again.

He could go and say hi—nothing wrong there—then go and find an informant to give him more details about the CEO of the Three Circles Recruitment Agency. There. That was an argument he couldn't find too many flaws in.

Sylvester sidled up to the demon. "Do you come here often?"

He felt like slapping a hand over his mouth straight after. Talk about cheesy pick up lines. But the male just quirked his lips in amusement. "Not really, no. I mostly live in the Human World."

Well, that was interesting. Only demons who had been resettled through one of the seven recruitment agencies could live in the Human World, so Mr. Handsome might know of Mr. Daemon. But it was doubtful that he'd know much.

"The Human World would be an interesting place to live, I bet."

A dark red eyebrow rose. "It has its perks."

Mr. Handsome finished his martini in a single swallow, and Sylvester's eyes were drawn to the sleek line of the male's neck. Auburn stubble marked the male's cheeks, and he looked good enough to eat. Literally.

Being a relative of the Incubi, sex was energizing for him.

"Did you want to see?"

Sylvester frowned, wondering if he'd zoned out for part of their conversation. "See what?"

"What the Human Realm is like? You can come visit my place." That deep voice had turned almost compelling.

"That's straight to the point."

"I don't believe in wasting time. It is, after all, the only real currency we have."

He was here on a mission; he shouldn't just leave without approaching his contact…. *You can always come back after.* Without meaning to, Sylvester stretched out psychic feelers, his mind searching for the motivation behind the invitation. But he brushed up against a solid wall, his Murmur ability blocked.

If anything, that made the demon even *more* sexy.

I won't be able to know what he thinks. Or what he feels.

It was the latter that normally had him high-tailing it out of apartments after a sexual encounter.

He grinned, a wicked tilt to the expression. "Well, then. Let's not waste a moment."

CHAPTER FOUR

Laird should know better than to allow the demon before him access to his home, to his body. But it had been a long time since he had relaxed, and now, with death looming over the horizon, he'd decided that it was time to have fun.

To be free.

And he had the distinct feeling that the male before him knew all about having a good time. At well over six feet, the demon was some sort of cambion, with chestnut hair and eyes so blue they reminded Laird of the sky over the Mediterranean. He wore a black leather jacket over a T-shirt and worn denim jeans. An air of danger lurked about him, which just made the male all the more appealing, if he was being fair.

"Well, then. Let's not waste a moment." Mischief shone on the cambion's face, a face which would have made the stone masons of ancient Greece weep from its beauty.

"Excellent." In fact, the more he thought about it, the more it seemed *right*. Hell, he was semi-erect just from talking to the cambion. Being on more intimate terms would only be better, he knew.

The cambion downed the rest of his wine quickly, leaving a drop of the liquid glinting on the edge of his lips. "Let's go."

Leaning forward, Laird pressed a kiss to the side of the demon's mouth, tongue licking away the missed wine drop. His skin electrified at the contact, his body humming with pleasure at the caress and at the taste of the demon. "Mmm."

Laird withdrew, watching as the cambion stood there, empty glass in hand, a slightly stunned expression on his face. A flash of lust seared through his blue eyes and the male's jaw tightened.

The cambion put the glass down on a nearby table with a click. "Ready?"

Triumph surged through Laird as he took hold of the cambion's hand. A second later, they were standing in the garden just outside his house, the glass-paneled mansion glittering in the moonlight. A dark forest lined the edges of the landscaped garden, while the crescent moon reflected in the glimmering surface of the pool.

A low whistle sounded. "Nice place."

"Thanks." He opened one of the glass sliding doors and led them inside.

"Whatever you do in the Human World, it must pay well." The demon glanced around the lounge area, with its U-shaped leather sofa and bar in the far corner. A fireplace hung suspended from the ceiling, a black egg-shaped iron hearth.

He gave a slight tilt of his head. "Better than you would expect."

The cambion turned to him then, the hard planes of his face shadowed in the silvery light. "What now?"

The directness of the question startled him, but it was refreshing. No obfuscation, no distraction. Just a straightforward question, asking for a straightforward answer.

"Sex, if you want it. Conversation and another drink, if not."

He wouldn't force the male to do anything he didn't want to—and he could, if he so desired. Murmur demons had the ability to make anyone do anything they wanted, through the art of mental suggestion. It was why they were feared almost as much as the Infernus, or worse, the Mortus; demons who could kill with the barest touch.

Those baby blue eyes darkened. "How about we make out for a bit, first?"

"We could do that."

They stepped toward each other, as if drawn, like magnets. Laird didn't know who reached out first, but his hand was on the back of the cambion's neck as the other male stroked a palm down Laird's back. Energy sizzled along his nerves as arousal began to pound through his blood.

Then their lips touched, the kiss scorching in its intensity. The cambion tasted like wine and lust. Laird's hand massaged the back of the other demon's neck. He angled his head to deepen the kiss, their bodies pressing together intimately. Smooth muscle and a rock-hard erection pressed against his groin, and he gave a low moan at the sensation, his skin on fire with a desire that burned from deep within. He looped an arm around the cambion's waist, pulling the male even closer, until he was overwhelmed by sensation.

A large hand slid down Laird's back, cupping his ass. Raspy breathing filled the air as the cambion pulled away, his lips red and swollen from their kiss. "You sure you want to keep going?"

Laird shook his head in disbelief. "Why would I want to stop?"

He hadn't felt this alive in centuries, he realized, as he swooped back in for another searing kiss. The cambion exuded vitality, strength, and raw sex appeal.

Life. He exudes life.

Something he'd been missing out on for years.

CHAPTER FIVE

Sylvester avoided the post one-night-stand walk of shame by simply teleporting out the demon's bedroom the next morning. He'd had a silent argument with himself over it, too. Stay and have breakfast with the other demon, or leave, and not risk the potential rebuff if Mr. Handsome didn't want to spend any more time with him. He'd chosen the latter.

Coward.

Maybe, but he didn't want to suffer a rejection before he had a coffee.

Back in his room at the guild, he showered, luxuriating in the hot water. While last night had been fantastic—the best sex he'd had in a long time, Hell, *ever*—he needed to get his mind back in the game. And if he really wanted to see the other demon again, well, he knew where the guy lived.

He toweled off after the shower and then shrugged into a new pair of jeans, T-shirt, and leather jacket. He strapped on a pair of Sig Sauer P229s, four knives, and a handful of distraction and sleeping spells—these in delicate pouches that exploded on impact. He'd revise his weapons list when he knew the exact kind of danger the CEO was up against.

I've never done bodyguard duty before in my life.

They had other specialists in the guild for that role, but none of them were immune from a Murmur's ability.

Hustling out of his room, he caught up with Trick in his office. The other demon was disgruntled, a fading sneer indicating his mood.

"Morning," Sylvester said. "I'm here to meet the client."

Trick gave a short nod, and then whipped out his iPhone, typing madly on the screen. A few seconds later, it dinged.

"We have to go to them." Trick shoved the phone back in his pants' pocket. Obviously his boss' mood hadn't improved overnight.

But there was a solution at hand. "Can we get a coffee on the way?"

A Tortas demon sat at reception, her large, limpid brown eyes focused on her computer screen. Her shiny white desk was decorated with a bunch of red flowers that looked a little too much like blood-dipped roses for Sylvester's liking. The rest of the room was spartan, with a few bucket-shaped chairs for potential clients, and a small table piled high with magazines. Hotel-style art lined the walls.

All in all, it was very tasteful, if a little…bland.

Trick cleared his throat loudly, causing the Tortas demon to snap her attention to them. "I didn't see you come in. Welcome to Three Circles Recruitment Agency, how can I help you?"

"We have an appointment."

The female frowned, then tapping something on her keyboard. "Oh yes, I see. One moment." She picked up the telephone and began speaking in a low voice.

Sylvester drank from his pumpkin spice latte and sighed. Great sex the night before with a stranger, a hot shower, and now a delicious coffee. Today was starting off well, despite the grump Trick was in.

The Tortas hung up the phone. "Mr. Daemon will see you now."

A glass door to their left opened, and they walked toward it. Once inside, the door swung closed, without any assistance from the occupant of the room. Sylvester quickly studied the area, noting the single entry, and the huge floor-to-ceiling glass panes that overlooked a bustling Manhattan—they were a huge security risk—and the sparsely furnished room.

His opinion of the building's security plummeted. The reception area could be accessed by lift or stairwell, and once there, the place was guarded by a single Tortas demon—a race not known for its hostility. When you were in danger, you wanted something like an Envio demon working security; they were huge, horned, and nasty.

Finally, his gaze landed on the client, seated behind his desk. Dressed in a dove gray suit, Mr. Daemon's expression was as calm and tranquil as a lake. Shock rooted Sylvester to the spot.

He knew that dark red hair, those piercing brown eyes, had seen that mouth open in ecstasy only hours before.

It was his one-night-stand.

Fuck.

His good mood evaporated in the blink of an eye. *You don't sleep with your employers.* That was a rule he lived by. Things just went badly when you mixed sex with work—unless that was your job, which was not the case. He didn't do 'honey pot' gigs, and he certainly hadn't ever screwed up this badly before.

How had he not realized the guy's species last night? He'd risked everything just for sex. Amazing, mind-blowing sex. But still….

Trick was speaking, so Sylvester shoved his turmoil to the back of his brain. He could deal with his colossal mistake later, when Trick wasn't around to find out.

"…while Sylvester does not normally do bodyguard work, he is ideally suited to this job."

Mr. Daemon nodded, his voice deep as he ocean floor. "Because I cannot read his mind."

"Uhh—"

An amused glint flashed in the demon's gaze. "I've already tried, and had no luck."

Did he know what kind of cambion Sylvester was? Was he a dead man walking?

"I assume the clause in the contract which states I can't harm your bodyguard is because of my species and his cambion ancestry?"

He knew?

"We know Murmurs don't like cambions," Trick said.

"Yes, although Murmurs don't like Murmur cambions. He doesn't have to worry."

Wait—he doesn't think I am a Murmur cambion?

Relief washed through him. Because while Mr. Daemon had signed away his right to harm Sylvester, the demon could still notify other members of his species. He could still end up dead.

But for now, it appeared he was safe for another day.

CHAPTER SIX

This…complicates things, Laird thought, staring at his new bodyguard.

If he'd known the cambion was going to be his new security officer, he wouldn't have slept with him. Wouldn't have had the most amazing sex of his long life. Wouldn't have woken up disappointed to find him gone. Wouldn't have agonized over going back to the bar to learn his identity.

Perhaps it is a good thing I didn't know.

From the chagrined shock in the cambion's—no, Sylvester's—eyes, his one-night-stand hadn't realized who Laird was, either.

Trick tugged his phone out of his pocket. "I have to go." The demon vanished.

"He was more talkative yesterday," Laird observed. He waved a hand, indicating that Sylvester should take a seat on the other side of the desk.

The cambion did so, twisting the coffee cup around in his hands. The scent of cinnamon reached him. "Trick's in a bad mood."

"I see."

It wasn't a great way to run a business—being moody with clients and staff—but then, assassination guilds tended to have slaves rather than employees. They couldn't just quit because they felt like it. And Laird wasn't exactly advertising his need for a bodyguard far and wide.

Sylvester stopped turning the coffee cup in his hands. "Sorry about last night."

Surprise had Laird clenching his hand in a fist. "What?"

"I don't sleep with clients. If I'd known—"

"They hadn't told you about the job yet?"

"They had, but they hadn't given me a damn photo."

He frowned. That didn't bode well for the competence of the Halcyon Guild. Then again, Laird had a habit of avoiding photographs because of his…disfigurement. "I see."

Sylvester flashed him a look. "Normally our files are so thick you have to read them over a week. But this was a rush job, so he just gave me the bare minimum. He probably thought I knew what all the CEOs looked like."

That was a fair assumption. There were only seven of them, and they tended to be well-known.

His confidence in the guild still wasn't high, however.

Although, he didn't doubt Sylvester's…prowess.

"The dossier said you had three guilds after you." He frowned. "The Lamia Guild, the Xargi and the Merry Men. Is that correct?"

"That is correct. I have not heard of any others being hired."

"Nor had we."

Sylvester crossed his legs, hooking an ankle over a knee. "The Lamia will come for you at night. They like stealth, and traps. The Xargi will use magic. As for the Merry Men…."

"They will do whatever it takes," Laird finished.

They were the worse of the three, although each guild was something to be wary of on its own. He would have to up the ante on his own protection spells.

Sylvester tapping his ankle. "You were an idiot. Last night."

"Excuse me?"

"Going out to a bar, when there was a hit ordered on you."

"I was at little risk." Even if there had been assassins waiting for him at the Casa de los Condenados, they would have had difficulty in succeeding in their mission. The place had been warded to the hilt with anti-violence spells—even his martini's flavor had been ruined by one. The second olive hadn't helped.

Sylvester snorted. "*I* could have been an assassin."

"I can take care of myself one on one."

He had for millennia.

"You're overconfident. That is going to get you—and possibly, me—killed. And I like living." Those baby-blue eyes flashed.

What kind of a cambion is he?

Laird probably should have wondered about that more, last night. But he'd been too wrapped up in lust to think clearly. Even now, he wished they were back at his house, rather than in his office, talking of death.

"I will defer to your judgement in his matter," Laird said.

Sylvester spluttered for a moment, then he grinned. It was breathtaking. "I thought I was going to have to argue more. Excellent. First things first, you won't be working here over the next few days."

"Excuse me?"

"This place is a security nightmare."

Laird studied his office. "It has one entry."

"And those massive windows. Some demons can fly."

"There are only two ways to get into the reception area."

"Which is guarded by a *Tortas* demon."

He did have a point there. Goldie was fierce when it came to administration, not warfare. But he had to have someone who could pass for human when needed—and Goldie was capable of casting illusions when confronted with humans.

"I can't just ignore my clients."

"You're the CEO, get someone else to do the interviews. You can work from home."

Laird was contemplating the arrangement when a high-pitched scream pierced the air. "Goldie!"

He leapt out of his chair and ran to the door, but Sylvester was already there. He shoved Laird back. "Get down on the ground, now!" Then the cambion was through the door, a gun in each hand as he confronted whoever dared terrify Goldie.

Laird dropped to his knees, ready to spring to his feet should the need arise. Gunshots and shouts shattered the air. It galled him, that he was to wait here, while one of his staff might be injured. But he was not stupid.

Not again, anyway.

If I had my godhood back, I wouldn't have to hide while others kill to protect me.

He stood. He couldn't do this any longer. He was not weak, not powerless. He was *still* a Murmur demon, the third most-feared species in all the Hells.

Sylvester shouted, "Clear!"

Laird was in the reception area a moment later. Goldie lay on her side behind the reception desk, dark green blood matted to her hair. He kneeled beside her, gently stroking her hair. "Goldie?"

Sylvester backed up to them, guns still held at the ready. "She's okay, just concussed."

He felt for her pulse anyway.

There.

Reassured she was alive, he stood, taking in the damage. Three dead Ulnak demons lay sluggishly bleeding on the hardwood floor, their orange skins browning with death. The door was busted open, and gunshots speckled the walls.

The place would need to be renovated. Again. Ulnak blood was like acid.

But there was nothing he could do about the dead. "We need to get Goldie to a healer, immediately."

Sylvester flicked him a glance. "I may know someone."

CHAPTER SEVEN

The Ulnak demons were from the Merry Men, they had to be, Sylvester thought. It was still daylight outside, so the Lamia wouldn't have attacked—that particular guild was solely populated by nocturnal species. And the Xargi…well, they usually brought a lot more magical firepower with them.

But this had been a lackluster attempt on Laird's life, if he ever saw one.

He would have done a better job, and he was thief. Mostly.

Sylvester stared down at the injured receptionist and then back at the Murmur. "I can't teleport you and the Tortas at the same time."

"I can look after myself," Laird replied.

Sure, because that was why he'd been hired in the first place. "I'll make a call." Stepping aside, he whipped out his cell and dialed.

"Sylvester?" The voice sent a pang through his chest.

He lowered his voice. "Hi, Mom."

"What trouble have you gotten into this time?"

"Not me, specifically."

"Who?"

"A Tortas demon."

"Is this a job?"

"Yes."

"I'll be there. Send me a photo of your location."

He took a picture and sent it through.

He had an awkward relationship with his mother. Full-blooded Pollus demons were relatives of the Incubi and had to have sex to survive. They were also generally only fertile with each other. Sylvester's conception had been a rather nasty surprise, but his mother had kept the pregnancy, and him.

She'd been shunned for it, as much as she could be, considering she was a cousin to the Pollus High Queen. But growing up, he'd never fit in, and had known he was the cause of his mother's discontent. So, when he turned seventeen, he'd left.

His mother hadn't approved, but she hadn't argued, either.

His mother teleported into the room. As a member of the royal family, she was stronger than most other Pollus demons, could travel to any Hell realm with ease. But she also charged for her healings.

He could understand that.

He got his mercenary tendencies from her, after all.

Her creamy skin shone under the electric lighting, while her red eyes scanned the fallen Ulnak demons, Laird, and the Tortus. She wore a sweeping navy-blue tunic, which was embroidered with serpents, the sign of her position in the Pollus hierarchy. Her coppery eyebrows rose. "We're in the Human Realm?"

"Yes."

Laird cursed. "You called a member of the royal Pollus *here*?"

"What?" Sylvester raised a hand, gun still clasped tightly. "She's only here to help the Tortas."

And how had Laird recognized his mother's position so quickly? Who *was* he?

More accurately, who had he been before becoming CEO of the recruitment agency?

His mother bent over the receptionist, pressing a gentle hand to her arm. "This is a mild concussion, but Tortas demons are prone to seizures after head injuries." She met Sylvester's stare. "I will take her with me. I'll send you the invoice."

She vanished, taking the receptionist with her.

He let out a relieved sigh.

Sylvester tried to keep work and family separate, he really did, but sometimes he needed the kind of healing help he couldn't provide. Oh, he would have been able to heal the Tortas, but he wouldn't have been good for much else, and he had to stay sharp. Using his magic tended to make him fatigued and spaced out for an hour or two after. He couldn't risk that at the moment.

Not when someone else's life hung in the balance.

Plus, his mother liked making money. It made her one of the wealthier Pollus, which helped her now he was gone.

Laird stared the Tortas' blood on the floor. "Why did you call a royal Pollus?"

He gave a careful shrug. "Because she's my contact."

"Hmm."

"How did you know she was royal?"

"I used to be one of Lucifer's Great Dukes. The Pollus High Queen lives in Inferno."

A Great Duke?

That would have been useful information to know.

I had sex with a former High Duke.

It was the same as if he'd gone and slept with Asha Himm, Hades' personal assistant. Stupid. Crazy. Insane. Liable to get him killed.

He inhaled slowly, trying to calm his racing heart. *He isn't a Great Duke anymore.* You're okay. But it was bad. It had been bad enough that Laird was a Murmur demon, but a former general in Lucifer's army?

That was even *worse.*

"Are you okay?" Laird reached out, placing a hand on Sylvester's forearm.

His whole body sprang to attention instantly, every nerve attuned to Laird's physical presence. Sylvester swallowed. "Just peachy."

"You're lying." The demon removed his hand.

"Just a lot to take in. You being a former Great Duke and all."

"Ah, that. It's why I don't tend to advertise it. It was a long time ago."

"That doesn't make me feel better. How long ago?"

"A thousand years."

"Cradle snatcher." The joke was out before he could think twice about it. He winced.

But Laird laughed. "When you are my age, it's hard not to be."

He's got a sense of humor.

Great. Now there was another thing to like about the Murmur.

I'm so fucked.

CHAPTER EIGHT

Laird watched Sylvester complete a methodical search of the corpses, hands moving so quickly they were nothing but a blur. *He probably started his career as a pickpocket.* Finished, Sylvester rubbed his palms together.

"No ID, no cash, nothing. I can't even tell which Hell-realm they are from. All signs seem to point to the Merry Men, but they tend to operate differently to this." The cambion frowned.

"From my contacts, they seem to prefer a coordinated attack," Laird said.

"And yet they sent three men."

"A diversion?"

"For what?" Sylvester tapped his fingers against a muscled thigh. "We should check your house. See if anyone has been there."

"I have wards. They would have let me know." Although, they were only as strong as he could afford, since he bought the place after he lost his godhood.

"Let's check anyway."

"I can teleport us there." He reached out and touched Sylvester's forearm, the contact igniting the simmering lust within.

There was just something about the cambion that made him *want.*

Laird concentrated, and then they were in his IM Pei-designed home. He'd paid a small ransom to get the famous architect involved, but it had been worth it. The clean lines, the way the property sat within its environment—all things that Pei had excelled at.

Sylvester withdrew his arm from Laird's grip. "The windows are a problem."

"How?" He'd always thought their size lent a sense of immersion to his home. That the glittering blue-lit pool just outside was, in fact, part of the house….

"They are easily shot down."

"These are reinforced glass, with magical wards." He wasn't a fool.

Sylvester withdrew a locket that hung around his neck on a thin chain and opened it. A dark gray powder lay within. It blazed with magic to his sight.

"A Clear Sight spell," Sylvester murmured, then dabbed the powder over his eyelids. It turned his baby blue eyes into a piercing azure.

"Ohh, these are good." He walked up to the glass and pressed a hand to the pane. "But they may not withstand a bazooka or missile launcher."

"They would use that?"

"The Merry Men would do anything to get the job done. I know we have those weapons in our armory. And if we have them…." He let the sentence trail into nothingness.

But Laird could fill in the blank.

Then they have them.

"I will up the protective wards."

"It will take more than that." Sylvester whipped out his phone and typed rapidly against the screen. "There, that should help."

"What did you do?" He lowered his eyebrows.

"You'll see."

Laird snorted. "Aren't you meant to be protecting me?"

"Of course. But I need to know what I have to work with, though."

The answer was vague enough to be irritating. Laird walked over to the bar in his living area, and then poured himself a Macallan, the amber liquid emitting a smoky aroma. "Did you want a drink?" He held out the crystal tumbler.

"I don't drink while I'm working."

He eyed the cambion over the rim of his glass. "A pity."

Sylvester rolled his eyes, but heat sparked within his blue irises. "Are you hitting on me?"

A little devil within made him say, "When have I stopped?"

Deep, rich laughter wove through the room, wrapping around Laird, warming him from the outside in. It was wonderful.

He took a sip of whiskey, the taste of peat and smoke dancing over his tongue in perfect harmony. Laird met Sylvester's stare, the tension in the room building, his skin electrifying with need. His Murmur ability reached out, to see if it could penetrate the cambion's mind, to know if the demon wanted Laird as much as he wanted Sylvester. But there was nothing there—Sylvester's mind impenetrable.

It only made Laird's desire skyrocket.

He took a step toward the cambion just as a protective ward sent a sharp jab of pain through his skull. His fingers clenched on the glass. All the im-mense power of his heritage rose to the surface of his mind. "There's a Foraci demon and an Imp here."

He would crush them.

No one threatened him, or his lover…. His power reached out and clamped over the minds of the two intruders. One fought back viciously—the Foraci.

"Ah, good. They were quick."

It took a moment for Sylvester's words to register. "You know them?"

"Yes, they're members of the guild."

Laird withdrew his ability, the tendrils of magic snaking back to him reluctantly. "You have a Foraci demon and Imp as part of your guild?"

"And not just any Imp. A Reynard's." Sylvester nodded at the wall of glass, where a tall female demon stood, her hair the color of wet blood. Slit-pupil eyes stared at him unblinkingly, while a green-gray-skinned demon stood at her side. The Reynard's Imp. With long, clawed fingers, and greasy black hair, he was not a pretty sight to behold.

And Reynard's Imps like to eat *everything*. Great. Lucky he didn't have any pets.

Sylvester strode to the nearest door and opened it, admitting the two other Halcyon Guild members. The Foraci stared at Laird, antipathy thick in the air.

Sylvester poked her in the arm. "Tone it down, Monica."

"He's a Murmur. You didn't say he was a Murmur. He tried to crush our minds."

"Oh, that's what the that was." The Imp scratched at his arm, which was scabbed. "Thought it might just be the ward."

"You got through my wards?" Laird asked, voice strangled.

The Imp turned liquid black eyes on him. "Yeah, like it was hard."

I'm a dead man walking.

CHAPTER NINE

Monica and Metcalf were the best-of-the-best when it came to bypassing wards—aside from Sylvester himself—so if they could do it, it was *possible* someone else could. It didn't mean that it was guaranteed, though. But the Merry Men didn't hire incompetent mercenaries. They could easily have someone as talented on the books.

Not that his ego liked to admit that.

But misplaced pride could get you killed.

Monica glared at him until he met her gaze and shrugged. Sylvester didn't need his Murmur ability to know she was angry at him for failing to tell her his client's species. Murmur demons and Foraci demons had been at war for centuries.

"I will do a sweep of the perimeter," she said, "to check for magical spells."

Metcalf's dark eyes shone like pools of ink. "I'll have a sniff around, see if anyone else has been on the grounds lately."

"Remember to capture them, not eat them," Sylvester said to his best friend.

"Can I take a little bite at least?"

Metcalf's goal in life was to try every flavor of demon to determine which one was his favorite. So far, he was deeply aggrieved that he'd been denied his chance at two Mortus cambions, as well as their boss, Trick, whose species was unknown.

He sighed. "Fine. But nothing vital, like the face, or near an artery."

"You and Peony ruin all my fun."

A sharp pang went through him at Peony's name. How was she surviving in her new home? Was she even still alive?

Worry about her later.

Sylvester handed his Clear Sight powder to Metcalf to use. The Reynard's Imp held it out to Monica, who shook her head, her mouth pinched in a thin line. "I can see magic just fine."

Metcalf pocketed the container, before catching Sylvester's glare. He dug it out and passed it back, although there was a tiny bit of pink flesh stuck to the back. Sylvester picked it off, and handed the slimy skin to Metcalf, who promptly ate it.

Gross.

After they left, Sylvester shut the door and turned back to Laird.

Both of the CEO's eyebrows rose. "A Foraci demon?"

"She can see magic, she has natural defenses against mental attacks, and she's powerful."

"And her species is also Hell-bent on exterminating mine."

"She is a mercenary at heart."

"I hope so." But Laird didn't look convinced.

Sylvester trusted Monica with his life—and he'd trust her with Laird's as well. She was all about the job first, and personal vendettas second. She was a lot like Peony's sister Dru, in that regard. Revenge didn't buy your freedom.

"They'll probably be a while," Sylvester said, watching them disappear into the gardens. The sun was a bloody orb as it sank toward the horizon. The Lamia Guild would be out to play soon, as well. "Why don't you show me the rest of your house."

Laird's voice dropped, "I can certainly show you around."

Sylvester fought the urge to chuckle. The demon was incorrigible. But the traitorous part of him enjoyed the attention—got a thrill out of knowing that Laird wanted him again, that last night wasn't just a quick fuck.

That they had the potential for more.

First you need to keep him alive.

CHAPTER TEN

Laird led the way through his house, showing Sylvester the varying rooms and spaces. They came to a stop in his office, and the cambion nodded at the wall. "What's behind there?"

Impressed, Laird muttered an incantation, and a door appeared. "My panic room."

"Cool."

"Did you want to check inside?"

"Of course."

Sylvester strode through the door like he owned the house, and quickly disappeared behind the portal. Laird followed close on his heels, eager to be near the other demon.

A low whistle sounded a moment later. "This room is warded to the hilt. You could survive a nuclear bomb here. One that went off in your house."

"It is the safest place I know of."

Sylvester turned to him. "You need to stay here from now on."

Laird glanced around the spartan room—there was nothing in here, aside from a naked bulb hanging from the ceiling, which illuminated the bare gray walls. "I would prefer to sit on my sofa."

The cambion glared at him. "It's going to be night time soon. The Lamia Guild will be out, and who knows what the Xargi are up to."

"I should be safe in my house."

"Hrm."

"You said the wards are strong."

"Yeah, but not strong enough."

"They just have to last long enough for my lawyers to close the loophole that Satan found."

Sylvester moved until he was barely a hairsbreadth away from Laird. Their exhalations comingled, and his skin turned electric. He could barely stand their separation—he wanted to feel the cambion's hands on him, to taste his skin, to—

"*Please* stay here."

Those blue eyes were so piercingly pure, so....

"Are you trying to sway me with you Pollus powers?" Laird drew away from the cambion, shocked that he could be manipulated that way. He was a Murmur, his mind should have been too powerful for such a trick.

Sylvester smirked. "Did it work?"

The cambion's expression eased the tension in his chest. "A little."

But was his lust for the other demon fabricated?

"Too bad." Sylvester shot him a sly glance. "And it wouldn't have worked at all if you didn't want me. I'm not an Incubus, after all."

At least the passion is real.

Too bad now wasn't the time to action it.

"I'm not going to stay here." Sure, he'd had the room built, but he had thought it would be for a partner, not himself. He was a former god, he could handle himself in a fight.

Sylvester crossed his arms over his muscled chest. "Once it's fully dark, we can do a better job of protecting you if you're here."

He sighed. The boredom alone might kill him. Although, he could *try* and convince Sylvester to stay with him while he was in the panic room. Surely that would make the time move faster. It would certainly be more enjoyable.

"Fine." Laird tilted his head to the side. "Let me get some things so it isn't so...dull."

They left the room. Once back in the living area, he noted that darkness had fallen outside. The pool glowed with blue lights in the night, and he strode to his warded windows, looking out over the shadowed garden. There was no sign of the Foraci demon, or the Imp.

A Foraci demon.

He would be in trouble, if other Murmur demons learned he had met one—and let them live. Foraci were only good as hostages, or dead. His people had been trying to exterminate them for centuries. Willbenders, it appeared, couldn't tolerate each other.

Personally, he didn't hold the same prejudices, but he wasn't the typical Murmur. He'd had to deal with other demons on a regular basis before he became a CEO, and now he couldn't afford to be prejudiced.

As he stared, a low boom echoed through the night, followed by light detonating in a fiery inferno on the glass wall next to him. The flames bubbled against the glass, expanding in a chaotic swirl of orange and red. A thunderous crack followed, the entire house shuddering from the impact of another missile. His wards screamed shrilly, but they held by the barest thread. Pain built steadily in his mind.

Sylvester's shout tore through the room. "Get down!"

A whistle pierced the hair next to his head, and the glass in front of him vanished.

Just disappeared.

What the—?

He dropped to his knees, in an attempt to make himself a smaller target. A hard body knocked him to the side. But it was too late—his chest exploded in agony.

CHAPTER ELEVEN

Sylvester shoved Laird to the ground as gun shots ricocheted around them. "Fuck. Fuckity, Fuck."

He should never have let him leave the damned panic room.

The Murmur demon moaned in pain. Sylvester rolled Laird over, his face blanching when he spotted the cavernous ruin of the other demon's chest. Blood and muscle, sinew and bone, they were all exposed in a gruesome display.

Murmur demons are strong.

He'd be able to survive this. *I just have to pack the wound. Once I deal with the attackers, I can then heal him.*

Sylvester couldn't risk doing it now, even though panic pounded through him with every beat of his heart. He'd be left weak, and he was now the last line of defense for Laird. He cupped the back of the other demon's head and frowned in confusion. Warmth pooled on his palm. Withdrawing his hand, he cursed at the blood there. Without thinking, he used his ability to assess the damage.

Half-destroyed heart. Pierced lungs. Shattered ribs. Severe brain injury.

He didn't know the medical language for it all, but he knew what it meant: Laird was dying. Murmur demons were their minds, and his had been brutally compromised.

No.

I can't let him die.

And not just because he was a client. There was something there…an attraction that needed to be pursued, understood.

"Sylvester!" Monica's shout had him turning away from Laird's shattered body.

The Foraci demon was sprinting toward him, covered in blood and soot, her face smeared with gore while her eyes glowed ferociously. She threw a blast of lightning-pink magic over her shoulder at an approaching behemoth. "Don't do it!"

How had she known my intentions?

"Cover me."

Her hand grasped his bicep, her slit-pupil eyes locking onto his. "He's a Murmur, his mind will lash out. You will die."

"I can't let him die."

"We're out numbered. We're doomed. Just get out of here. Leave the body."

But Sylvester shook his head, the refusal immediate. "No."

She hissed, spinning around, two blades appearing in her hands. "It's your funeral. But I'll stay for now."

The last thing he heard was Metcalf letting out a whoop of joy somewhere in the darkness. Then his power began flowing into Laird, forcing the stuttering—failing—heart into beating once more, healing the shredded brain tissue first.

You will not die. I won't let you.

A mind clamped down on his, one so powerful that everything went blank.

❖

Monica growled low in her throat as Sylvester collapsed over the Murmur demon.

A heartbeat passed, and then a telepathic wave shot out, making her knees wobble, and her head pound. She gritted her teeth through the pain. "I warned him."

"Warned who?"

She spun on her heel, blades up as she took in a new arrival. He stood next to Sylvester and the fallen Murmur, his black hair swept away from delicately pointed horns, and pale pink eyes glowing with power.

"Who the fuck are you?" she demanded.

But she knew what he was. A Murmur.

"My name isn't important."

"Come to finish the job?" She jerked her head at the supine Murmur.

"No. I came to avenge my uncle. We felt his call."

His uncle?

She looked over her shoulder, and fifty figures suddenly appeared in the yard, each silent and still as a poised cobra. The swarming mass of the Merry Men—partnered with the Lamia Guild and a couple of Xargi—froze.

She swallowed against a suddenly dry throat.

The newcomers were all Murmurs.

I am going to die.

"I am here to protect him." She jerked her chin at Sylvester.

A casual flick of those rose-quartz eyes. "They are both dying."

Her eyes flashed with her power. "Well, you'd better get to avenging, then."

"Yes." He grinned, a slow cruel expression that spoke of carnage and joy. "I hope we meet again." Two short swords appeared in his hands, as if conjured there, while he strode out to the battlefield.

Bending down, she grabbed Sylvester's phone from his pocket, and hunted through his contact list until she spotted the number she was after.

Hopefully it wasn't too late.

CHAPTER TWELVE

Warmth flooded his body in a steady stream, only to disappear just as quickly. *Where is it going?* He followed the pulse of heat, startled to see it was funneling straight into Laird, through some sort of tele-pathic connection. *I'm a channel.* How he was gener-ating such healing power, he had no idea. But would it be enough?

The powerful mind that had slammed into his own began rifling through Sylvester's thoughts, his memories, his very…. A moment later, a door opened in his mind, a bright white light beyond beckoning him.

Is this death?

Never go to the light.

But he couldn't stop himself; his mind was drawn like a moth to a flame. A moment later, he was through the portal, and within a landscape that was both stark and beautiful in nature. Sharp lines of smoky quartz, smooth expanses of sand, glimmering glass balloons of thought. The sound of rolling thun-der echoed in the distance, while the air smelled like charged ozone—as if lightning were moments away from striking.

"You made it."

Sylvester turned at the voice and stared.

It was Laird.

But not as he'd ever seen him before.

His horns shone golden, his cheek was unscarred, and his being shone with light. He was so beautiful, it hurt to look upon him.

"What *are* you?" He stepped closer, unable to maintain a distance, even though part of him screamed that Laird was dangerous.

"This is my true form. How I used to be."

"And that is?"

"Not important anymore."

"You're dying."

"*We're* dying."

But Sylvester wasn't so sure. The healing energy was still pouring into him; his body was still alive.

He closed the distance between them, until it was physically painful to look at the Murmur's radiant beauty. Reaching out a hand, he touched Laird's body. Energy sparked between them, and his heart stuttered, before evening out, before syncopating with the Murmur's before him.

A hard shell locked around his mind—not a pris-on, but something…protective. A telepathic con-nection that had formed unbidden….

Before the word could form fully in his conscious-ness, Laird's mind opened to his. Thousands of years' worth of knowledge, pain, happiness, melancholy; they flooded Sylvester, until he didn't know who he was anymore, until he knew Laird as well as he knew himself.

Not Laird. Baal.

His lover was a fucking *god.*

The question was blurted, "What happened?"

Laird raised a hand to Sylvester's cheek, his arm shaking. "We're mates."

Pure Murmur demons had their one fated mate… but he was only a cambion.

Hurt flickered in Laird's eyes. "Is that a bad thing?"

Sylvester grabbed his hand as it withdrew. "No, I just never thought…."

His brown eyes lit with amusement, as Laird re-alized Sylvester's true ancestry. "You kept a secret from me."

As Sylvester studied the golden glow. "So did you."

A warm chuckle laced the air, and peace filled him.

This was right.

This was meant to be.

Then he woke up.

CHAPTER THIRTEEN

Everything hurt.

I ache too much to be dead.

Laird raised a hand to his head, shocked that he was able to move at all. He was flat on his back, Sylvester draped over his chest, the cambion's hand clutching Laird's shoulder in a death-grip. Right at this minute, he couldn't imagine a better way to wake up.

He's my mate.

The word felt strange, unreal, but so utterly right. He'd never thought he would have one, his mind too powerful for a regular Murmur. How had Sylvester survived the bonding?

Wait. *How* had they bonded?

He's part Murmur.

But that wouldn't have been enough to allow the mating. Sylvester's mind should have been destroyed by the force of it.

"You're awake."

He turned his head toward to the speaker—careful not to move Sylvester. Shock sizzled through him as the female Pollus demon from his office came into view.

He asked the first thing that came to mind, "How is Goldie?"

"You should be asking about how my son is, rather than your assistant."

Son?

Her gaze dropped to Sylvester.

Her son.

"Sylvester is a *royal* cambion?"

"He was never formally acknowledged, but yes."

"Why do you help him, if he isn't legitimate?" The Pollus were sticklers for their hierarchy and honor.

She squatted down and ran a gentle hand over the back of Sylvester's head. "I am his mother. He is mine to help." Her expression turned fierce. "I felt him dying. I was coming for him when someone messaged me to say he was in trouble. If not for me, and my connection to the queen, Sylvester would be dead. You would have killed him."

Now he knew how they'd both survived the mating.

Without Sylvester's mother's connection to the queen—and hence all of the Pollus race's healing ability—they'd have both died.

"He's my mate."

"That's a Hell of a bonding ceremony you have." She stood.

"Mine is not…typical."

"When will Sylvester wake?"

"Soon."

A new voice intruded. "Uncle! You're not dead!"

Laird turned his head, confused at the sight of his sister's grandson. Midnight black hair, rose-quartz eyes…Magnas. Twin blades were held in each hand, both covered in blood and gore.

"No, I am alive," Laird said, running a protective hand over Sylvester's back.

"We heard your death call."

"I was a bit precipitous."

"Well, I guess people can get dying wrong." But the look on his face said otherwise. Magnus had always been too clever for his own good. His nephew shot a curious look at Sylvester, and Laird's ability rose protectively.

"I am mated. This male is not to be harmed."

Magnus grinned—his teeth were bloodstained. "And a god again."

"What?"

He withdrew into his mind for a moment, hunting for the power that had been lost to him for a millennia. There, blazing in gold, was his godhood.

Whole. I feel whole again.

But he didn't know if that sensation was from the return of his godhood, or the discovery of his mate.

Would he be forced to give up his power again?

I won't do it. If I'd had this power, I never would have been at risk from Satan in the first place.

He might have been captured by the Hell-lord once and tortured, but it would never happen again. Plus, he was stronger now.

"That explains much," Sylvester's mother said.

A low groan emerged from the cambion, and Sylvester raised his head. "We're alive!"

"Yes."

They both moved simultaneously, mouths pressing against each other in triumph, in laughter, and most of all, in knowing. When they'd mated, their secrets had been laid bare, their desires and fears.

"Get a room!"

They pulled apart. The Foraci demon stood with her arms crossed over her chest.

Sylvester looked around them, then groaned into a sitting position. "Where'd all the Murmur demons come from?"

"We came to avenge Uncle. Even though he didn't die, we still avenged him."

"And you're still here?" Sylvester turned to the Foraci.

"They didn't manage to kill me. Some tried." She barred her teeth.

Magnus' gaze slammed into the Foraci, but she didn't seem to notice.

"So, what happened to the other guilds?" Sylvester raised a hand to his head.

"They're gone. For now."

We need a plan, he thought.

"Don't worry," the cambion turned to him. "I'll think of one."

EPILOGUE

Laird had spent a week living amongst the Murmur stronghold, with Sylvester visiting him whenever he could. At their arrival, Sylvester had been met with grim-eyed hatred, but they'd left him alone. Magnus, it seemed, had delighted in the uproar. But as a mate to the most powerful Murmur alive, the other demons knew better than to mess with him, impure blood or not.

There had been quite a few discussions as a result.

On the upside, since he'd mated with Laird, when no one else had been strong enough, cambions appeared to be currently off the 'kill at sight' list. Despite Monica's efforts in saving Laird, the Foraci were still in the number one place, with her name right up there.

He'd tried to put in a good word for her, but that had only appeared to annoy them even more.

Cantankerous bastards.

And if he thought the Murmurs were bad…well, Mortus demons were even worse. Normally, Sylvester wouldn't have gone anywhere near their den out of a sensible fear for his life. But what do you know, he'd visited twice now in a week. This time, Peony was hopefully going to save his butt.

Well, his and Laird's.

"Sylvester! You made it." Peony rose from a seated position behind a stone desk, her near-white hair glowing in the flickering candlelight, and her golden skin smooth with health. She looked good. Really good. Better than the last time he'd seen her, when she'd been attacked by a hoard of Infernus demons, here in one of the Mortus den's great halls.

He grinned. "No one tried to kill us on the way down."

They'd been met by a Mortus guard at the entrance to the den, his black hair swept up into a manbun, and his eyes a cold gray. He'd stood to the side of the door once they'd entered Peony's office.

"And this is your client?" She turned curious eyes on Laird, who was muting his godhood with all the power he had. They'd decided it was best to hide his power's return, at least until the Satan situation was sorted.

"Yes, and my…mate." It still felt strange to say the word—strange but wonderful.

Peony smiled, her face lit with true happiness. "That's wonderful!"

How had she managed to become the Mortus queen and still retain her…innocence?

She was a doctor—and a damned good one at that—and somehow, she'd murdered the former Mortus king, taken his throne, and kept the Mortus in line, all within a week. He could only hope that her powers of persuasion could extend to his current problem.

The door opened, and a freaking *angel* strode into the room. He still couldn't get used to it. And he'd known Z for weeks. Laird coughed slightly in surprise, even though he already knew about the fallen angel. The only times their species met was on a battlefield. To have one living in Hell—and mated to the Queen of the Mortus, no less—was nothing short of a fairy tale.

"So, you have a favor you want repaid?" Z came to stand behind Peony.

"Yes.…"

❖

They stood hidden from view within an invisibility spell cast by Laird. Peony and Z were behind the stone desk, Peony with a metal crown adorning her head, a computer on and glowing with impatience. Satan teleported into the office, his arrival accompanied by the tolling of bells.

So, this is the Hell-lord.

He was on the taller side, with obsidian eyes that reminded Sylvester of hungry sharks. His mahogany hair was slicked back from a pronounced widow's peak and power hummed through the room. Sylvester was way out of his league here: Satan, Peony—who was now super-powerful—Z, and Laird. He was the weakest link.

As if sensing his thoughts, Laird reached out and clasped Sylvester's hand, the contact searing in its simplicity; its affection.

"Granddaughter." Satan closed the distance to the desk, sitting in one of the free chairs available.

"Grandfather."

Sylvester turned to Laird and mouthed 'Granddaughter?'

The Mortus are direct descendants of Satan. It's a form of respect. Laird's voice flowed through Sylvester's mind, the words tasting of thunder and rain.

"You said you had something urgent to discuss with me?"

"Yes. I want you to rescind your order that Mr. Daemon, CEO of the Three Circles Recruitment Agency, is to be killed."

Amusement sparked in Satan's dark eyes. "I have ordered no such thing."

"You suggested that this was something you would favor."

"I would never be so direct."

"Then you can *indirectly* pass the information on that he is no longer a target."

Satan crossed his ankle over a knee, his pose carefree, as if he were just humoring Peony. "Why would I want to do that?"

The Mortus queen gave him a grim smile. "Because I know who ordered the hit. If you don't rescind it, I'll have them killed."

"Come now, you're a pacifist."

"But my twin sister is not. And I will kill to protect what's mine."

Satan's mouth compressed into a thin line. "You already have a mate. Who is the CEO to you?"

She leaned forward. "The CEO is very important to me. The Mortus need an avenue to expand, and he will provide it."

"There are six other recruitment agencies."

"But none with his…personal abilities."

Is she hinting at your godhood? Sylvester asked.

She shouldn't know…but I am a Murmur, and even the Mortus tend to treat us with respect.

"So, this is a business arrangement?"

"Everything is business, Grandfather."

The Hell-lord barked out a laugh. "You are very much of my blood. But since I didn't order the hit…."

"If it is not called off within twenty-four hours, the current mastermind dies. If another steps into their place, they will die, too."

"You can't possibly know these identities. I don't."

Liar.

"I have this." Peony opened a drawer and withdrew a glass sphere. Inside the globe, green and black flames flickered, licking at each other before swirling away. Sylvester fought the urge to whistle. She twirled the sphere in her hand. "Odin's Orb."

Satan scoffed. "No demon can use it."

She put the Orb away. "I'm not a full demon."

"What do I get out of this?"

Peony met his stare unflinchingly. "Your henchmen's survival."

"That is not good enough."

"Do you want the Mortus to move against you?"

They can do that? Sylvester asked.

I didn't think so, Laird replied. *But look at Satan.*

The Hell-lord's expression had grown pinched, less assured. "I'll remember this." He stood.

She gave him a slow smile. "I would hope you do."

Satan disappeared.

With the Hell-lord's departure, relief spread through Sylvester, making him almost giddy with triumph. Laird placed a hand on his shoulder and squeezed. Affection, lust…and something that felt a lot like love, burned through Sylvester. They'd done it. Laird was free. And they were going to live.

This was the first day in the rest of their lives.

I am glad I am your mate, Laird whispered into his mind.

Same.

Laughter, rich with joy sparked through him.

Peony turned in their direction. "There, it is done."

The spell vanished, leaving them visible. Sylvester stepped forward. "Would you have really killed them?"

A troubled expression flickered over Peony's face. "I was hoping it wouldn't have to come to that. We have dungeons here. I could make them 'disappear.'"

Sylvester nodded. He wanted to hug Peony to show her his appreciation, but one bare touch of her skin, and he'd be dead. He hoped she could see the emotion in his eyes. "Thank you."

"I didn't do this just for me. You're going to have to go back to the Guild and tell Trick that he has to employ my cousin."

"Piece of cake." He waved a dismissive hand through the air. But in reality, he wasn't too sure how Trick would take the news. But a deal was a deal. And no other mercenary guild could boast the services of a Mortus. It would be a strategic win, provided said Mortus didn't kill any of the other guild members if they annoyed him. Hopefully Trick would be okay with the arrangement.

After a second round of thank yous, Laird and Sylvester teleported back to the Murmur stronghold. In Laird's palatial rooms at the fortress, Sylvester kicked off his boots and sank onto the sofa, groaning with satisfaction as the chair molded around him. "I think we won."

Laird settled next to him. "We did. I live to see another day."

They kissed, but it was an expression of pure emotion: joy.

Pulling away, Sylvester stroked Laird's cheek. "So, what do I call you now? Baal or Laird? Since your godhood is back."

"I stopped being Baal a long time ago. Laird is my chosen name."

"Perfect." Sylvester grinned, loving the feel of the man next to him, the sensation of Laird's mind hovering protectively against his.

Laird may be a god, but their bond was equal; *they* were equal.

"I hate having to admit that I will need to thank Satan at some point," Laird said softly, stroking a hand down Sylvester's arm.

Sylvester thought he'd misheard. "Thank him?"

"If not for the attack, we might have not seen each other again for centuries. We may have never ended up mating. I would not have known this… love."

Love.

Sylvester had never said the words to a partner before, but he knew, deep in his bones, that he loved Laird, and would grow to love him more every day. And because of their bond, Laird knew it, too.

Leaning forward, Sylvester placed an affectionate kiss on the Murmur's cheek. "We would have found each other again. Matehood, is, after all, fate."

And fate had chosen perfectly.

They were partners.

Forever.

Copyright © 2019 by Amanda Pillar.

Our columnist, Julie Pitzel, has been a receptionist, radio DJ, bill collector, telemarketer, administrative assistant, community college instructor, and an expediter (a.k.a. professional nag). She's been involved in the Houston writing community for many years including two years as president of a local Romance Writers of America chapter. She writes paranormal fiction from a geodesic dome south of Houston, where she lives with her husband and a pair of cats. Most recently, her story "The Dance" was published in The Death of All Things anthology.

YOU READ *THAT?*: VAMPIRES AND OTHER LOVERS

by Julie Pitzel

I love stories about witches, vampires, shapeshifters, and haunted houses. Ever since I discovered macabre stories in the Scholastic catalog, I've been hooked on reading horror. I'm not sure when I first became aware of paranormal romances. Until I joined Romance Writers of America in the mid-nineties, the only romances I read were thick and sassy historicals. I rarely paid attention to any of the other romance subgenres, and probably missed a lot of novels I truly would've enjoyed.

The first paranormals I remember reading mostly involved witches, time travel, or ghosts. There were some vampires, but in those stories the vampires were the villains—not the romantic leads. Looking back through literary history, I wondered when did vampires and shapeshifters move from being monsters to leading men?

In 1819 John Polidori spent that infamous summer with Lord Byron and the Shelleys. While Mary invented science fiction, Polidori penned *The Vampyre* and introduced the world to the bewitching predator, Lord Ruthven. Ruthven was a departure from the vampires of myth and lore. He wasn't merely a slavering monster, he was a suave nobleman who seduced his victims before killing them.

The vampire as a member of the nobility carried over twenty-six years later with Sir Francis Varney (aka Varney the Vampire) from *The Feast of Blood*, and of course fifty years after that with Count Dracula. These early male vampires had money and status.

Though they presented themselves as nobility and were easily accepted into polite society, they were monsters on the inside. They destroyed their victims and their victims' families without care. Mostly. Varney at least hated his condition and professed remorse. He eventually killed himself at the end of 232 serialized chapters. Those three characters defined vampire legends and invented many traits that we still see in literature and movies today.

They were seductive, but they weren't romantic. Surprisingly, the closest we come to a paranormal romance among the classic vampire tales is Joseph Sheridan Le Fanu's *Carmilla*. Published almost thirty years before *Dracula*, it has a lesbian romance at its core. Being a Victorian gothic, the protagonist's father and his vampire-hunting friend must save her from Carmilla's depravity, although they couldn't save her from the depression of losing her first love. So, still not a romance, but Carmilla is at least portrayed as having feelings for the protagonist.

Jump to the 1970s and we have Anne Rice's *Interview With A Vampire*. Rice's vampires are introspective and not just out for a quick bite. They aren't soulless villains like Ruthven or Dracula. But still, there's more lust than love to them. Then in 1978, Chelsea Quinn Yarbro published *Hotel Transylvania* with Count Saint-Germain and—in my humble opinion—paranormal romance was born. Saint-Germain is thousands of years old and only requires a little blood to survive. He cares for and protects the mortals in his life and doesn't indiscriminately turn others into vampires. Not all of the Saint-Germain stories are romances, but he's definitely a leading man.

Looking at shapeshifters, the only classics I can think of are *The Strange Case of Dr. Jekyll and Mr. Hyde*, and the 1941 movie *The Wolf Man*. They are both tragedies, with the main character unable to control his alternate identity. Not very romantic. Most classic werewolf books and movies are either gruesome and tragic, ala *American Werewolf in London*, or campy like many of the Universal monster movies pitting the Wolf Man against Dracula or Frankenstein or helping Abbott and Costello. In 1994, when *Wolf* came out with Michelle Pfeifer and Jack Nicholson, the idea that a werewolf wasn't inherently evil was novel. Nicholson's character is told

the wolf is only as wicked as the man and it's a revelation. This is the first prominent werewolf romance I can think of that doesn't end in tragedy or a cure. And within a few years there were several books and series with good werewolves (including an excellent series by Alice Borchardt, Anne Rice's older sister).

Paranormal romance and its sister-genre, urban fantasy, exploded in the late nineties and beginning of this century. During that time we were introduced to a wide range of paranormal heroes and heroines and a lush assortment of stories involving vampires and shapeshifters and other supernatural characters. Some were moody and intense while others were rom-coms with a twist.

The first Southern Vampires book with Sookie Stackhouse, came out in 2001. I'd never heard of Charlaine Harris and didn't know anything about the book. But I remember finding it on its own cardboard display at a local bookstore, and I had to buy it. It had humor and intense action with a quirky, smart, and resourceful heroine who still managed to get herself into predicaments. Finding these stories was significant to me. Up until then, I hadn't seen many books that could interweave horror and humor. This was not only what I wanted to read, it was the type of story I wanted write as well.

So many groundbreaking series started about that time, it's difficult to point to any one and say "This is it. This started the trend." Many new conventions were introduced with this new batch of supernatural icons. They created their own rules. Some vampires were born instead of created, werewolves could control their shifts and didn't have to change with the full moon, witches were a separate subspecies—the list of changes from the mythos of *Dracula* and *The Wolf Man* is extensive. But as long as they were consistent, readers accepted the changes.

Readers more than accepted paranormal romance and urban fantasy. They embraced the genres, giving into the spell like Lucy Westenra giving it up to Dracula. An article I read from 2010 briefly states that some stores saw a thirty percent increase in paranormal romance sales. The numbers have died down since 2010—at least major publishers aren't putting out as many now as they were ten years ago—but it's still a solid, well represented genre. And though we can look at the history of the last two hundred years and see the progression from monsters to tragic heroes to major love interests, I can't explain why. Maybe the surge of popularity tied in with 9/11 and war and wicked rulers here and abroad. Possibly, most paranormal/urban fantasy stories contain an element of good versus evil. Or maybe the uptick was because we needed the escapist fantasy. There's a good argument it was a combination of both. I can only say that I always liked a good vampire story and now I can get that with a side of hot romance as well.

C.S. DeAvilla writes award-winning science fiction, fantasy, and romance under another pen name. She has been a romance fan since she sneaked a peek at her mother's massive historical romance bookcase and fell in love with all the characters. She reads every romance genre—as long as two people are falling in love, she'll give it a read. Her favorite authors are Jennifer Crusie, J.R. Ward, Darynda Jones, Suzanne Brockmann, Sarah MacLean, and Kristan Higgins. But she always has room for one more.

RECOMMENDED BOOKS

by C.S. DeAvilla

Title: ***Jock Rule***
Author: Sara Ney
Publisher: Three Legacies
ASIN: B07L4YT48Y
Release Date: December 4th, 2018

Sara Ney mentions in her author's note that *Jock Rule* gave her some trouble while writing, but I couldn't tell that while devouring this story. Kip Carmichael is a hairy beast of a dude. Rugby player. Not interested in a relationship, not interested in women, period. Not anymore. Fed up with women only wanting him for his family's money, Kip had resigned himself to the single life through college. Cue Theodora (Teddy) Johnson awkwardly getting tossed aside by her jock-hook-up seeking friends at a Jock Row party. Kip instantly is fascinated by her attempts to seem like she belongs there. He decides to help her by giving her a few pointers and she surprises him by making it clear she's not there to hook up. Soon they're both ditching the boring party scene in favor of one-on-one hang outs at Kip's house so Teddy can avoid walking in on her hook-up-addicted roommate and snuggling close when the heater goes out. As always, Ney's new adult book gave me the warm tingles as the main couple found their way to each other and resisted as long as they possibly could (maybe even beyond that). I'm a huge fan of slow burn and this book hit the spot. Ney's books are filled with funny quips, snappy dialog, and lots of sparks of chemistry. Each of her series books are better than the last and the *Jock Row* series is shaping up to be my favorite.

Title: *The Risk*
Author: Elle Kennedy
Publisher: Elle Kennedy Inc.
ASIN: B07G4H3665
Release Date: February 18th, 2019

Elle Kennedy's hockey romance books are everything I love about sports romance in a college setting. The team banter back and forth like actual siblings— there's a close bond that's unbreakable even among the ones who don't seem to get along. And above

all: honor and loyalty. All in a setting where emerging adults are experimenting and learning about how to be autonomous. Brenna intrigued me from the first book in the series; reformed bad girl, Briar University coach's daughter, and general badass with hockey stats. She's caught the eye of their rival team, Harvard, and is currently, casually seeing one of the players until the team captain forces his teammate to call it off. The athlete does it easily and Brenna doesn't like the power display, so as a show of dominance she tracks the captain down and gives him a little taste of her revenge. Jake Connolly isn't satisfied with just one bite though and can't help himself when she suddenly needs a favor from him so she can score her dream job at a sports network broadcasting company. Jake, already signed with a major league team when he graduates, promises to take her on a fake date to make her look more important to her potential boss. But only if Brenna will go on a real date in exchange. The bargain is struck, and we all know how this trope will play out: both of them hot for each other and a real problem considering they're sworn enemies playing on opposing teams and her father's grudge against Harvard's team. The conflict in this one is thick, and it doesn't let up as these two characters fall for each other despite all the reasons they should stay away. I always know Kennedy will give me a good read and this second installment of the series keeps the quality high and promises future books will be just as tantalizing.

Title: *99 Percent Mine*
Author: Sally Thorne
Publisher: Harper Collins Publishers
ASIN: B075WXBG13
Release Date: January 29th, 2019

After *The Hating Game* sensation last year, I couldn't wait until Sally Thorne's next release. I was not disappointed with *99 Percent Mine*; I had the same exhilarating feeling while reading it. Darcy Barrett has a problem with her heart: it skips and hesitates, and she's been sick since she was born. Her one-minute older twin brother took away her chance to be born first and possibly heart-defect free. And her heart has definitely not been the same since she let her ideal man and best friend down. Tom Valeska is Darcy and her brother's shared best friend. She figures Tom is maybe ten percent hers? Twenty? It fluctuates day to day, but he could have been one hundred percent hers when he told her he loved her. But she freaked and ran away to Europe. Once she decided it was okay to love him too, she came back to find him dating a perfect homemaker of a girlfriend. Didn't take long for them to be engaged and Darcy's heart to slip further into pieces. But now she has a second chance. Tom is once again newly single and remodeling her grandmother's home. Darcy has every chance to win him back, but he's seemingly not interested in getting his heart broken either. Both of them dance around each other and hide any growing feelings each might harbor from Jamie, Darcy's brother, until they can't manage to pretend much longer. This is a roller-coaster of a will-they-won't-they love story that keeps you rooting for all the characters and also wanting to hit them upside the head for allowing things to get so complicated. But emotions are never as cut and dry as we'd like, so fiction isn't any different. *99 Percent Mind* will enchant you the same way *The Hating Game* did and then we'll all be waiting another year for Thorne's next installment.

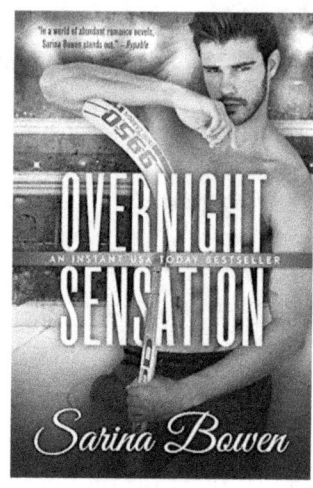

Title: *Overnight Sensation*
Author: Sarina Bowen
Publisher: Tuxbury Publishing LLC
ASIN: B07K5WL48S
Release Date: January 22nd, 2019

I'm a bit of a fangirl when it comes to certain authors and Sarina Bowen is one of those writers who just knows how to keep me enthralled. *Overnight Sensation* is the next book in the Brooklyn Bruisers series—a hockey romance you know you want to break open this spring. Heidi Jo, the hockey commissioner's daughter, should be off limits to every hockey player in the league, but Heidi has a weakness for the big guys on skates and one in particular has a weakness for her. Jason Castro lost his high school sweetheart in a car crash six years ago and he's sworn off relationships since then. Instead he's made his life all about the sport and getting ahead, but lately he's not been doing well in that either. A friendship with Heidi is the best distraction from losing his touch on the ice. Once deemed the overnight sensation, he'd settle for any crumbs of luck he can get. And Heidi quickly becomes his lucky talisman, but he's also falling for the girl who manages to be everywhere at once, jumping through hoops to show her father she can work any job in the rink—nothing is beneath her. Her zest for life reminds him of what he's been missing and the two make a perfect pair. I have to admit, there were a few teary moments in this book that had me unsure if Castro would be able to open up to Heidi more than just a surface level, but Bowen manages to deliver a good story all the way till the end.

Title: *The Unhoneymooners*
Author: Christina Lauren
Publisher: Gallery Books (Simon and Schuster)
ASIN: B07MGS7HF1
Release Date: May 14th, 2019

If there was ever an author that I *knew* I could count on, it's Christina Lauren. Her books have a certain feel to them; while I'm reading I know I'm in the hands of a talented storyteller. Or storytellers—since Christina Lauren is the pen name for two writers working together to tell the tale. *The Unhoneymooners* is a delightful addition to their list and sure to be an instant bestseller. Ami Torres is the luckiest gal around—winning contests and sweepstakes—enough to fund her wedding and honeymoon. But her twin Olive Torres is the unlucky one. It seems for every burst of fortune that comes Ami's way, and equal opposite reaction of misfortune swoops into Olive's life. Or so Olive believes. But Olive's (bad) luck takes a turn when the entire wedding party and guests fall ill after the (free) shellfish buffet is infected with a toxin. Now there's a (free) non-refundable honeymoon and Ami begs her sister Olive to go in her place and assume her identity. The catch? The groom's brother Ethan Thomas, the only other guest who escaped

the shellfish disaster unscathed, is to be her guest. Can't have a (free) honeymoon sweepstakes winner without a groom! Olive isn't excited about having the overly cautious and judgmental Ethan along for her one shot at something good finally happening to her, but she vows to not let his gloomy presence get in the way of her good time. Except Ethan isn't the person she expected, and she finds herself warming to the brother of the groom and realizing her sister isn't as lucky as she appears. The twists of this book were set up from the beginning and although anticipated, the authors deal with the fallout in unique ways. There are consequences to Olive's lack of honesty, and it really sucks because as a reader I recognized Olive's desire to be as honest as possible, even though the entire premise of her good luck required her to lie. Everyone has experienced that moment in life where you attempt to take a shortcut to success, and it ends up coming back ten-fold. Watching Olive and Ethan's budding relationship get hit after hit was painful, but also makes for a really entertaining read. Conflict, and there is a ton of that in this book, keeps these pages flipping at a clipped pace. I was upset to see I'd reached the end and now must wait for the next Lauren book to grace my e-reader again.

Andrea was drawn to Chicago to the famed Charlie Trotters Restaurant. There, Andrea was exposed to one-of-a-kind wine cellar in which she received one of the best wine educations in the world, tasting & serving some to the most rare and most special wines ever produced. She worked with some of the world's top ingredients, Chef's, Farmers, food lover's and wine aficionados, but homesick, Andrea returned to Santa Fe, NM, where she was Partner & Head Chef at Rasa Juice Bar & Ayurveda. Andrea received many rave reviews and won the Local Hero Award two years in a row for her organic, plant-based café. Her attention to detail to her beautifully plated and delicious food is enhanced with the love and care she infuses into every bite! She is currently the Owner and Chef of The Temptress Private Chef & Catering operated out of her home town of Santa Fe, NM.

THE TEMPTRESS PRESENTS: COLD PRESSED GREEN LEMONADE

by Andrea Abedi

Juicing has many benefits for the body and mind. It is a great and easy way to get nutrients into the body and is easy to digest. When we drink juice, our digestion does not have to work so hard to break down these nutrients. When this happens we get these vitamins faster and easier in our body. Juicing vegetables and fruits can give your body energy, get you an easy way to get vitamins and minerals and fiber. Go ahead and juice, your body will thank you for you it!

INGREDIENTS

3 organic pears-3
2 organic lemons, peeled
3 whole romaine greens
2 cucumbers
½ inch piece fresh organic ginger
1 bunch fresh kale

DIRECTIONS

1. Fill a large stockpot with 8 cups of distilled water.

2. Take pears and cut out the core and the seeds, leave the skin on, set aside.

3. Slice off skin of lemons, discard skin and set aside peeled lemons.

4. Cut off the base of the romaine bunches, discard roots, slice lengthwise so it is easier to process through juicer.

5. Slice cucumbers leaving skin on and cut lengthwise.

6. Peel off skin on ginger with a spoon, discard skin and set fresh peeled ginger aside.

7. Take the kale leaves and peel the center vein out.

8. Gather all ingredients that have been cleaned and process all through a juicing machine. Strain if you want a smoother juice.

9. Taste and if needs more sweetness add ½ a pear.

Enjoy!

xo

Copyright © 2019 by Andrea Abedi.

CLOSING EDITORIAL

by Lezli Robyn

I write this on the Sunday evening where so many lovers in the world are curling up on the couch together to watch the last episode of *Game of Thrones*. If you ever wanted evidence of how much an impact authors can have on their readers (and George R.R. Martin is arguably one of the best writers), you only have to read the many news articles, blogs posts, Facebook comments (and memes) and Twitter reactions to the last few episodes of GoT to know that the elements a writer can create with their fiction—the worlds they set their stories in, the unique characters we grow endlessly fascinated with, and, most importantly, the relationships we love to ship—can really reflect back to us what we want out of life. And for the most part, that is a happily-ever-after. It's what we all yearn for, instinctively.

And what better genre to offer a happy ending than the romance genre? I have curled up with many a romance novel, devouring the happily-ever-afters to help nourish my heart and remind it that the right person is out there, if you keep yourself open enough to find them. And *Heart's Kiss* is dedicated to not only giving you one HEA, but at least five an issue, guaranteeing to leaving you feeling all loved up with the many possibilities and forms love can appear in your life.

So, as we approach summer in the United States—I'm looking forward to long walks on the beach with my chiweenie, Bindi—and winter in Australia and varying forms of each around the world, I thank our readers for supporting us in our labor of love, this magazine. We couldn't have done it without you! Until next time, lovers.